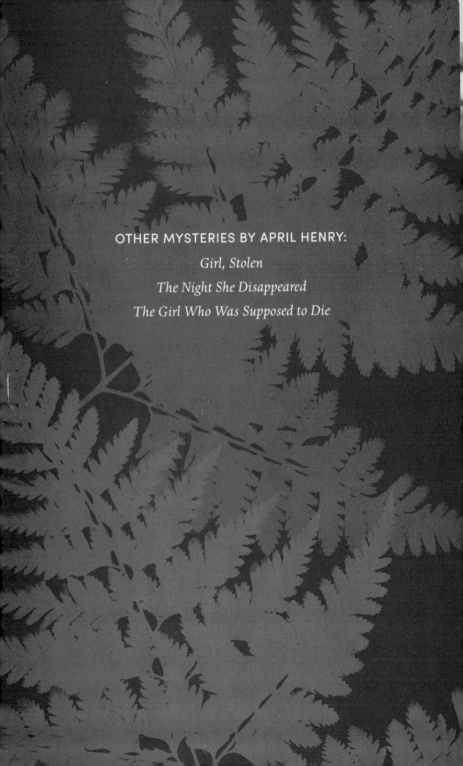
OTHER MYSTERIES BY APRIL HENRY:

Girl, Stolen

The Night She Disappeared

The Girl Who Was Supposed to Die

POINT
LAST
SEEN

THE
BODY
IN THE
WOODS

APRIL HENRY

Christy Ottaviano Books

HENRY HOLT AND COMPANY • NEW YORK

Henry Holt and Company, LLC
Publishers since 1866
175 Fifth Avenue
New York, New York 10010
macteenbooks.com

Library of Congress Cataloging-in-Publication Data
Henry, April.
The body in the woods / April Henry. — First edition.
pages   cm. — (Point last seen ; 1)
Summary: While helping the Portland County Sheriff's Search and Rescue to seek
a missing autistic man, teens Alexis, Nick, and Ruby find, instead, a body and join
forces to find the girl's murderer, forming an unlikely friendship, as well.
ISBN 978-0-8050-9852-5 (hardback)
ISBN 978-0-8050-9866-2 (e-book)
[1. Murder—Fiction. 2. Criminal investigation—Fiction. 3. Friendship—Fiction.
4. Eccentrics and eccentricities—Fiction. 5. Mystery and detective stories.]
I. Title.
PZ7.H39356Bod 2014   [Fic]—dc23   2013046396

Henry Holt books may be purchased for business or promotional use.
For information on bulk purchases, please contact Macmillan
Corporate and Premium Sales Department at (800) 221-7945 x5442
or by e-mail at specialmarkets@macmillan.com.

First Edition—2014
Designed by April Ward
Printed in the United States of America

1 3 5 7 9 10 8 6 4 2

BLOOD

FOR ALEXIS FROST, NICK WALKER, AND RUBY McClure, it all started with a phone call and two texts. It ended with fear and courage, love and loathing, screaming and blood. Lots of blood.

When the classroom phone rang in American history, Alexis Frost straightened up and blinked, trying to will herself awake as the teacher answered it. She managed to yawn without opening her mouth, the cords stretching tight in her neck. Last night had been another hard one.

"Alexis?" Mrs. Fairchild turned toward her.

"Yes?" Her heart sped up. What was it this time? The possibilities were endless. None of them good.

"Could you come up here, please?"

Mrs. Fairchild was looking at Alexis as if she was seeing her in a new light. Had it finally happened, then, the thing she both feared and longed for? Had something happened to her mother?

———

Nick Walker's thumbs were poised over the virtual keyboard of the phone he held on his lap. He was pretending to listen to Mr. Dill, his English teacher, while he was really texting Sasha Madigan, trying this angle and that to persuade her to study with him tonight. Which he hoped would mean lots of copying (on his part) and lots of kissing (on both their parts).

The phone vibrated in his hand. Mr. Dill was busy writing on the board, so Nick lifted it a little closer to his face. It wasn't a reply from Sasha but a message from his Portland Search and Rescue team leader.

Search in Forest Park. Missing man. Meet time 1500.

His first SAR call-out! He jumped to his feet.

"Nick?" Mr. Dill turned and looked at him over the top of his glasses. "What is it?" Mr. Dill had a lot of rules. He had already complained about Nick's habit of drawing—only Mr. Dill called it doodling—in class.

Nick held up his phone while pointing at it with his other hand as if he had been hired to demonstrate it. "I'm with Portland Search and Rescue, and we've been mobilized to find a man missing in Forest Park. I have to leave now."

"Um, okay," Mr. Dill said uncertainly. Someone in Wilson High's administration had had to sign off on Nick being allowed to join searches during the school day, but maybe the information hadn't filtered down to his teachers.

No matter. Nick was already out the door.

He just hoped someone from class would tell Sasha. A text wouldn't do it justice.

Nick Walker, called out on a lifesaving mission.

Ruby McClure felt her phone buzz in her jeans pocket. She waited until the end of chemistry to check it.

Fifteen hundred made so much more sense than three P.M. Ruby preferred military time. No questions about whether "nine" meant morning or night. No having to rely on context. No one getting hung up on whether 1200 had an A.M. or a P.M. after it, which was a ridiculous idea because A.M. meant "ante meridiem" and P.M. meant "post meridiem" and *meridiem* was Latin for "midday," and twelve noon was midday itself.

It was 1357 now. Which meant she had an hour to get home, change into hiking clothes, pick up her SAR backpack, and meet the rest of the team at the Portland sheriff's office.

Piece of cake.

Ruby pulled out the keys to her car as she walked to the office to sign herself out. On the way, her phone buzzed again. It was Nick, asking for a ride.

A BUNCH OF TEENAGERS

THE PORTLAND COUNTY SHERIFF'S OFFICE had called out all teams to search for the missing man. Of the twenty teens on Team Alpha, twelve had responded. Now they climbed out of the fifteen-passenger van driven by Jon Partridge, one of the adult advisers, and into a parking lot next to Forest Park. Team Bravo, along with the sheriff's deputy assigned to this search, were in a second van and would take the other end of the huge park. With the exception of the deputy, everyone was a volunteer.

The last one out of the van, Alexis was surreptitiously trying to eat a granola bar from her backpack's emergency rations. Today was looking like it might qualify as an emergency. Not because of this search, but because of how the apartment had looked when she stopped to grab her gear. By the time Alexis had gotten off the city bus at the sheriff's office, the van had been idling outside. She had been the last to board.

Mitchell Wiggins clapped his hands. "Listen up, people!" Mitchell was an Eagle Scout who wanted to be a cop. Even though he had been elected team leader only a few days ago, it was clearly a natural fit. He seemed born to wear some kind of uniform. His yellow SAR climbing helmet—the yellow marked him as the leader, while the rest of the team wore red helmets—was already buckled into place. Now his pale, earnest face regarded each of them in turn. "Today we will be conducting a hasty search for a thirty-four-year-old white man named Bobby Balog."

This was it, then. The real deal. Alexis took a deep breath. Most of the other teens here were certifieds. They had completed the nine months of training and had been called out on dozens of searches. All Alexis and a few of the others had behind them were seven Wednesday-evening classes and two weekend training exercises. From class, she knew that a hasty search was just like it sounded, a quick search that stuck to the most obvious trails and routes. It was also quite possible that this would turn out to be what was known in SAR circles as "a bastard search," when you went looking for someone who was never really lost in the first place.

"Bobby is five foot eight and two hundred pounds," Mitchell continued. "He's wearing dark blue Nike shoes. The sole pattern is made up of squares about the size of keyboard keys." A few of the more experienced kids, who had training in tracking, nodded. "He's also wearing jeans, a gray sweater, and a navy blue windbreaker."

Alexis exchanged a look with Nick. She knew they were thinking the same thing. Not a single bright color. This wasn't going to be easy.

"And he's autistic," Mitchell added, putting the icing on the cake. "The PLS"—point last seen—"is his bedroom, which is a mile from here, but he loves Forest Park and has run away and hidden here before."

"How autistic?" Ruby asked. "That diagnosis covers a wide range of behaviors." She was standing right next to Alexis. Too close. As usual.

Alexis slid a half step sideways. She didn't want anyone thinking they were really friends. Most especially Ruby.

Mitchell was opening his mouth to answer when a silver Lexus sped into the lot. Before it was even at a complete stop, heels were clip-clopping toward them. Their owner was a woman with short, curly dark hair who wore a tailored long black wool coat. Smeared mascara rimmed her red, swollen eyes. Following more slowly in her wake was a silver-haired man dressed in dark slacks, a white shirt, and a black sweater vest. He was coatless, even though the temperature was only in the mid-forties.

"Wait a minute." The woman stopped short when she saw their faces. "*You're* Portland Search and Rescue?"

Mitchell pulled his skinny frame to its full six-foot-two height. "Yes, ma'am, we are."

"A bunch of teenagers?"

"Marla." The man laid his hand on her arm, but she shook it off.

Jon cleared his throat and stepped forward. He might be twenty-six, but Jon had been in SAR since he was fifteen. "Every person you see has volunteered to be here. Most of us have received hundreds of hours of training and conducted dozens of rescues. That's why the Portland County Sheriff's Office chooses us to search for people who are lost or injured." His steel-gray eyes never left the woman's face. "Now, we could keep talking about their experience level, or we could start searching for your son while there's still light."

Mrs. Balog blinked and closed her mouth.

Only Ruby was unfazed by this exchange. "Exactly how autistic is Bobby?"

It was Mr. Balog who answered. "He doesn't have any physical handicaps or other medical conditions. He's a fast walker and not much of a talker. He'll probably hide from you."

"He loves the woods," Mrs. Balog said. "And he doesn't like strangers." She ran a knuckle under one eye. "He's done this twice since we moved to Portland, but the other times it was summer."

Alexis wished they still had summer's long days and warm temperatures. Instead it was November and they were working against time, against the sun that was already sinking, against the night that would drop temperatures even further, against the creeks and fallen snags and rabbit holes that Bobby might blunder into.

Regaining his professional balance, Mitchell turned his focus back to the team. "Remember, guys, your job is not just to search but to inform the public. Let them be your eyes and ears. If they have anything to report, they can do it at the command post we'll set up here."

"I have a photo of Bobby," Mr. Balog offered, pulling a cell phone from his back pocket. His face was creased and worn. Alexis wondered how many of the lines were the result of having a kid who wasn't normal. But you couldn't change your family.

Mitchell took the phone and looked at it for a long moment before passing it on. As it went from hand to

7

hand, Alexis was reminded of the few times her mom had taken her to church, the Communion tray passing in silence. Mrs. Balog shivered as the wind began to pick up, and her husband put his arm around her.

When it was her turn, Alexis cradled the image of Bobby's round face. His smile was strangely wide and flat, as if someone had instructed him to show all his teeth, top and bottom. She silently promised him that she would find him if she could.

Jon's phone rang, and he walked to the other side of the van to answer it. For a second, Alexis strained to hear, wondering if they had found Bobby, but it sounded like he was arguing with his girlfriend. While Jon was busy, Mitchell split them into teams of two or three, assigning the more experienced searchers the higher probability areas. Each team was given a rat pack—a small pack that buckled across the chest and contained a GPS and a radio.

Finally only Alexis, Ruby, and Nick were left to be dispatched. Obviously Alexis should have taken another step away from Ruby while she still had a chance.

Jon came back around the corner of the van. "Where's the rest of the team?"

"Already out on the trail," Mitchell answered.

Jon dropped his voice so the Balogs couldn't overhear. "What were you thinking? These three are brand-new! You should have split them up."

They all looked down the trail, but the others were already out of sight.

Mitchell's face reddened. "Sorry!"

Jon sighed, rubbing a spot just above his left eyebrow. "It is what it is." The Balogs were leaning in, trying to listen, so he lowered his voice slightly. "I don't want you three out of sight of the trail or each other. Nick, you'll be in charge of the rat pack. Ruby, I want you to take the topo map."

Leaving nothing for Alexis. She had tried her best to fit in, but maybe Jon could see right through her.

SAR was her ticket to college. She wasn't going to be like the other girls in her neighborhood, getting pregnant or dropping out or settling for a minimum-wage job. But even a state school would be expensive, and her guidance counselor had told Alexis that her B average was not enough to win her any scholarships. To make herself stand out, the counselor had said, she needed to add an eye-catching extracurricular. But Alexis was too uncoordinated for sports, she couldn't read music, and yearbook had been too competitive.

It had been either this or the Mathletes.

Mitchell handed the topo map to Ruby, and the four of them leaned in close. His long finger traced the way they were supposed to go. "Follow this section of the trail."

"But that's nowhere near where you said he was found the last two times," Nick protested.

Mitchell's jaw clenched. "We need to cover ground, and figuring out where he isn't is almost as important as figuring out where he is. So you guys had better get going."

Suddenly Mrs. Balog grabbed the arm of the blue Gore-Tex jacket Alexis had scored a few weeks ago at Goodwill. "Do you think you'll find him?" Her breath was hot and stale. Alexis couldn't look away from her brown eyes, the whites threaded with red.

What should she say?

"We're going to try."

LONG YELLOW TEETH

"WE NEED TO GET GOING BEFORE IT GETS too dark," Ruby called back to Alexis. Ruby was already twenty feet down the trail, buckling the dark red climbing helmet over her crimson hair. Nick wasn't far behind. Alexis gently pulled her arm away from Bobby's mom and followed. For the first few hundred yards, the trail was paved and ran parallel to a stream.

As soon as they were out of sight of the adults, Nick clambered up on a huge fallen log half covered with pale green, velvety moss. He was still carrying his helmet by its strap.

"You're supposed to stay on the trail," Ruby said.

Only when he came to the end of the log did he jump down, landing in a puddle with a splash. Alexis rolled her eyes. Nick was like a big kid sometimes. All he wanted was attention, any kind of attention.

Tweet! Tweet! She jumped at the sound of his whistle. The blast jolted her back to the reality of their search.

"Bobby!" Nick called out. "Bobby!"

"It's not logical to be calling his name," Ruby said. "His mother said he would hide."

"What difference does it make?" Nick shrugged. "You saw where he went before. We're not going to be the ones to find him."

Even though he was probably right, Alexis was still careful not to hurry as she called his name and blew her whistle. Remembering their training, she looked up, down, and sideways to be certain they didn't miss either Bobby or a piece of clothing he might have discarded. She even turned around to look back. In her head, she heard Jon's voice. *Lots of evidence gets missed because it's on the back side of a tree or a rock, and people forget to look behind them.* Knowing they were looking for a real person made Alexis's breath come a little faster. It was like walking into a haunted house and waiting for a bloody man to jump out brandishing a rubber ax.

In this part of the park, the trees grew straight as pencils and the branches didn't begin until many feet over their heads. Beams of light slid between the trunks, looking as if they should be illuminating a miracle instead of a patch of undergrowth. The shadowed ground was carpeted with yellow-green grasses and bright emerald ferns. They were surrounded by a million shades of green: khaki and jade, olive and lime and avocado.

Tiny waterfalls silvered the stream, and birds trilled in the trees. It was all like a fairy tale. And bad things happened in fairy-tale forests. Witches and wolves lay in wait. Alexis shivered.

"Are you cold?" Ruby asked. "I have an extra jacket you could borrow."

Of course she did. It was probably some solar-powered thermal item. Ruby was a gear nerd, and her parents bought her REI's top of the line. Alexis got stuff on Craigslist or at the Army-Navy Surplus store.

"That's okay. I'm good."

Like Ruby's clothes would fit her anyway. Alexis was built like an Amazon. Every PE teacher she'd encountered practically drooled when they saw her, imagining her on the basketball court. But Alexis had zero coordination. At most she could manage three of anything: two hands and one foot, two feet and one hand. Add the fourth, especially if it was supposed to do something different from its partner, and she was lost.

"Bobby!" Alexis shouted again, and Nick joined in after a few more blasts on his whistle. "Bobby!"

As if in answer, two labs—one black and one yellow—appeared on the trail ahead. They bounded toward the three of them, nosing crotches and putting their muddy paws on knees. Looking at their long yellow teeth, Alexis shrank back. The dogs in her neighborhood would as soon bite you as look at you. Nick laughed and rubbed the black one behind the ears. As she petted the yellow one, Ruby's grin transformed her narrow, foxlike face.

"They're friendly!" came a shout from farther up the trail.

A guy in his mid-thirties, wearing black shorts and a gray T-shirt, appeared behind the dogs, his hiking boots slapping the sludge. Mud flecked his bare calves. He glanced curiously at their red helmets—Nick's still wasn't on his head—but he didn't slow down. The dogs broke free to run ahead of him.

Alexis, Ruby, and Nick looked at each other. Somebody had to speak, so Alexis did. "Hey, wait, hold up a sec."

He did, jogging in place.

"So we're with Portland Search and Rescue." It was hard not to feel like an impostor. She remembered Mrs. Balog complaining that they were just a bunch of teenagers. "Have you seen a thirty-four-year-old man, kind of heavyset, wearing a navy blue jacket and jeans? He's lost."

"He's not lost," Ruby corrected her. "He's autistic, and he's probably hiding."

"I've seen lots of people," the man answered, "but no one like that." And then he was sprinting down the trail, calling to his dogs.

"If you do see him," Alexis yelled after his back, "tell the people in the main parking lot."

Fifteen minutes later, they came to a branch in the trail. After consulting the topo map, Ruby said they should take the path to the left. They passed a curve and saw a heavyset man walking toward them. He looked like he was in his early thirties, with a round, shaved head. Over one shoulder, he had a big blue duffel bag. He glanced at their red helmets and then away. For the millionth time, Alexis wondered if they really needed to be red.

"Hello," Ruby said. "We're with Portland Search and Rescue. Has anyone asked if you've seen a thirty-four-year-old man who is five foot eight and two hundred pounds and autistic? He is more than likely hiding."

His gaze flicked over each of them. "No. Definitely not." He was already edging past them. Alexis wondered if Ruby's stilted way of speaking made him nervous.

"If you do see him, note his location," Ruby said. "He probably won't approach you. There's a command post set up at the end of the trail, and you could report it there."

"Sure." He threw the last word over his shoulder.

The next person they met was a homeless guy in his early twenties. His black dreads ended in white and black beads shaped like skulls. He was smoking a cigarette, and his fingernails were outlined in dirt. Ruby's nose wrinkled, but it was Alexis he watched impassively as she explained about the search for Bobby. He said only two words: "no," when asked if he'd seen Bobby, and "okay," when she told him about the command post. Then he walked on.

While Alexis and Ruby were still speaking to the homeless guy, Nick kept walking. He disappeared around the bend, but they could hear him calling occasionally. Hadn't Jon told them to stick together? Alexis and Ruby kept moving up the trail, all the while scanning the undergrowth, the ferns and shrubs and saplings, the rocks and fallen trunks.

The problem with looking, Alexis thought, was that you might find someone. Maybe the reason Bobby wasn't answering wasn't that he was hiding.

Maybe he was hurt.

Maybe he was dead.

Her breath came shallower.

There! What was that? Just off the trail. Her heart started to race, but it turned out to be just a small brown spiral-bound notebook. Alexis leaned over and picked it up, flipped through the pages. The first half was filled with tiny crabbed cursive handwriting, the kind she associated with old people, as well as a few line drawings.

The back pages hadn't been used yet. One side of each page was blank, and the other was lined.

"It's a birder's notebook." Ruby leaned in. "Bird-watchers use it to record what they see." With one of her chewed-down-to-hamburger fingernails, she pointed at an empty lined page. "You write your observations here—what the bird was doing, what time you saw it, where it was, if there were other birds with it, if it was feeding—and then you draw it on the blank side."

Alexis was just thinking that whoever owned it wasn't a very good illustrator when a man's voice called out from behind them.

"Oh, good, you found my notebook."

They turned. A white-haired man with silver-framed glasses and a full white beard hurried toward them. Take away his cargo pants, binoculars, and camera, and add a red hat and suit and another fifty pounds, and he'd make a pretty good Santa Claus.

Alexis put the notebook into his outstretched hand.

"Thank you so much!" He slipped it into the pocket of his black North Face jacket. "I realized I must have dropped it last night when I was looking for a northern spotted owl. I thought I would try retracing my steps."

"A northern spotted owl?" Ruby stopped in her tracks. "Are you serious? It's been years since one's been here."

"There are rumors one's been sighted."

Her eyes narrowed. "Are you sure it wasn't a barred owl?"

The older man's face lit up. "You must be a fellow birder! I'm hoping to put a northern spotted owl on my life list."

"I have a strong interest in birds," Ruby said. "Also in continuity errors, true crime, and gum flavors."

Could Ruby get any weirder?

"There's a lot I'd like to put on my life list." The birder patted the pocket with the notebook. "A lot."

Here was her chance to get them back on track. "I'm afraid we're not looking for birds," Alexis said. "We're with Portland Search and Rescue, and we're looking for a missing man." It was getting easier to say. "His name's Bobby Balog. He's thirty-four, about two inches shorter than me, and two hundred pounds. He might be hiding."

The man frowned. "Is he a criminal?"

Alexis shook her head. "No. He's autistic and afraid of strangers."

"I haven't seen him." He turned to go back down. "But I'll keep an eye out."

After he was gone, Ruby cupped her hands behind her ears—which made her look even more bizarre—and turned her head from side to side like some kind of bat. "I can't even hear Nick anymore," she complained. "Mitchell said we were supposed to stick together."

"It's not like he can get lost as long as he stays on the trail," Alexis said. This was Forest Park, and while it might be five thousand acres, it was still in the middle of a big city.

"I think we should catch up," Ruby said.

"If that's what you want to do, go ahead. I'm going to keep at this pace."

Ruby hesitated for a moment, then hurried past her.

Two months ago, Alexis and Ruby had been close. Well, as close as Alexis let anyone get. On orientation day, the meeting room had held four girls, twenty-three boys, two women, and three men. Normally Alexis wouldn't have had anything to do with Ruby, but she had felt lost in an ocean of boys. Alexis and Ruby got tighter after one girl and then a second dropped out.

But the more Alexis got to know Ruby, and the more Ruby tried to get to know Alexis, the more Alexis had realized she would really rather not be friends. Not when Ruby asked so many questions. She didn't need Ruby finding out the truth about her life and blurting it out to the next person she came across.

Alexis rounded a corner and almost got run over by a long-haired guy on a mountain bike.

"Hey, stop!" she yelled, but he kept going. "We're looking for a missing man!" she called to his retreating back. Had he even heard her?

Alexis looked around. She was completely alone. Then her eyes found a shadow that wasn't quite natural.

The curve of a back. Lying motionless in the ferns.

UNIMAGINABLE FEATS OF BRAVERY

NICK HAD LOST SIGHT OF RUBY. LOST SIGHT of everyone, really. Occasionally he remembered to blow his whistle and call out Bobby's name, but he did it with less and less enthusiasm.

What was the point of even pretending to look for the guy? They had been given the least likely section of the park to search. Basically, this was a training exercise, and not a very interesting one. How could you find someone if there was no one to be found? There was zero challenge. It wasn't like having to build a fire and keep it going throughout the night, or being told to fashion a shelter with only the materials you had at hand. There was no chance that they would be the ones to find Bobby.

Nick had joined SAR to prove himself. People at school saw a skinny kid who couldn't sit still, a kid who couldn't stop talking, a kid who didn't fit in anyplace, but Nick knew that, just like his dad, he was capable of unimaginable feats of bravery.

If only he was given the opportunity.

Which was where SAR came in. Boy Scouts? Please.

He did not want to earn little cloth badges. He wanted to do something real. In SAR you not only learned skills, you also saved lives.

Except not today.

Nick's mind kept starting to wander, and after a while, he let it. His body might be in Forest Park, but instead he imagined he was in Iraq. Back where his dad had been.

In his mind's eye, he saw piles of gray rubble. A car burnt down to its blackened bones. A bleating goat. White buildings, sand-colored roads, oily smoke. A woman all dressed in black, not even her eyes visible. A world without color. Certainly nothing green.

His red climbing helmet, which he had finally strapped on after Ruby wouldn't shut up about it, became a combat helmet. His SAR backpack was now military issue.

He whirled around and aimed an imaginary rifle. *Blam*!

His mother never mentioned his dad, but Nick had seen the medal, snug in its case, in his mom's dresser drawer. A Bronze Star on a red, white, and blue ribbon. He had looked it up on Wikipedia. "Awarded for bravery, acts of merit, or meritorious service."

But his mom never talked about the medal or the man. His dad had died in combat—that was all Nick had been able to piece together from cryptic comments made over the years. Sacrificed himself to save others.

Nick had been four when his dad died. Were his few memories even his? Or did they come from movies? From his imagination? A deep voice, big hands lifting him up under his armpits, a scratchy cheek against his own.

All his mom ever said was, "The army destroyed your father. You'll join up over my dead body."

When joining up was the only thing Nick wanted.

In the army, he was sure he would feel like he belonged. He had a weird pale Afro and was too light skinned to be black, too dark skinned to be white. Nick had grown up in a white world, but he didn't really fit there. That world didn't really want him. He'd seen people from his mom's work clutch their purses until they realized he was her kid.

Portland was segregated, not in ways that anyone talked about or even admitted, but it was still unusual for him to see another black person on the streets of Southwest Portland. In a lot of his classes at Wilson, there were white kids, Hispanic kids, Asian kids—and Nick.

But in the army, what mattered was being fast and strong and brave. And Nick was all those things.

Tweet! Tweet! Tweet!

He was so lost in his daydream that for a minute, he didn't know what the sound was, or even where he was exactly.

Tweet! Tweet! Tweet!

And then he did.

It sounded like someone had found Bobby.

And it hadn't been him.

Nick set out in a long-legged lope, running back down the trail toward the sound. Was it Ruby or Alexis? It didn't seem fair that he might have walked right past something important, something they had spotted and he hadn't.

Maybe Nick hadn't been the one to find Bobby, but he still might be able to help. Bobby was a big guy. He could be injured. He could be unable to walk, and he might need to put his arm over Nick's shoulder so that Nick could walk for both of them. Or maybe Nick would have to make a travois the way they had learned on a training weekend. He could drag Bobby to a clearing where they would wait for a helicopter to set down, the rotor wash whipping up dirt that would sting their eyes.

In another minute, Nick would realize his fantasies were exactly that.

SOMETHING AWFUL LURKING

N*O, ALEXIS THOUGHT. NO, PLEASE. I'M NOT seeing this.*

But she was. It was a back. A human back, clad in a black jacket. The hump of a shoulder, a dip, the smaller hill of a hip.

From this angle, she could not see the legs or the face. All she could see was the back.

Unmoving. Half curled around a bush.

Her blood chilled.

It was him. Right there. The missing man. For a minute, Alexis couldn't even remember his name. Everything inside her was blank. Holding its breath. As if as long as she didn't remember, time wouldn't heave itself forward. Because if he was there, right there, and not moving, then Alexis would have to do something.

And she was all alone. She looked around to make sure this was true. No one on the trail before or behind her. The only sounds were the wind sighing through the trees and the birds calling.

She forced herself to open her mouth. It was so dry,

her lips made a smacking sound as they parted. And as they did, his name came to her.

"Bobby?" The sound was lighter than a whisper.

Alexis forced a swallow past the lump in her throat and tried again. "Bobby?"

A little louder. Shaky.

The back did not stir.

Alexis tried again, putting some steel into it. "Bobby?" It was still not quite a shout, but it was loud enough—it had to have reached him. After all, he was only about thirty feet away.

He didn't move.

Her heart hammered in her chest, in her ears. Alexis fought off a wave of nausea as her stomach rose up and crammed into the back of her throat.

Maybe he was unconscious. Maybe he had hit his head on a tree limb, or broken his ankle and passed out from the pain.

Maybe.

Bobby's parents had said he had no medical problems. And it wasn't like there was anything out here that could kill him. Just trees and small streams, trails and under-growth. But he was a big guy. Maybe he had had a heart attack. Maybe it was even possible that he had gotten tired from his big adventure and lain down for a nap.

Alexis was going to have to go up to him. Lean over. See what was wrong. The feeling that gripped her now was the same one she had had as a little kid, the one that told her something awful was lurking underneath the bed, just waiting to reach out and grab her ankle as soon as she was within reach.

Alexis was going to have to get close enough to touch him.

No matter how afraid she was.

And then she remembered the whistle in her hand.

Three blasts, wasn't that what they had said in class? Three blasts, pause, and then three more. And anyone in SAR who heard it would come running.

Alexis put the whistle to her lips and blew. It came out breathy and light, no louder than the birdsong above her.

Deciding that first one didn't count, she tried again, putting all her fear behind it. And again. And again.

Tweet! Tweet! Tweet!

If Bobby was conscious, shouldn't he have moved at the shriek of the whistle? But he lay still.

Tweet! Tweet! Tweet!

Nick would know what to do. He was always talking about how his dad had been in the army. On one of the training weekends, he had been the first to figure out how to use a branch as a splint. And Ruby's parents were doctors.

But Alexis couldn't just stand here until Nick and Ruby showed up. She forced her feet to start moving. Toward that curved-away back.

Shouldn't she be able to see the ribs expanding with each breath?

If he wasn't breathing, did that mean he was . . .

Her stomach bottomed out. Her steps were so small she was nearly walking in place.

And that jacket—why was it black, not navy blue as Bobby's mother had said?

Although, according to their instructors, civilians frequently got important details wrong. Clothing colors, shoe size, medical conditions—all things that were vital to search and rescue personnel, and all of them likely to be muddled, confused by the very people who were so anxious that you find their missing loved ones.

Alexis was now only fifteen feet away. She couldn't bring herself to call out Bobby's name again, as if he were a sleeper she was trying not to wake.

The thing was, as she got closer, she could see the top of the head. And the hair on that head.

It wasn't brown and short. It was blond and longer. At least shoulder length.

And that dip in the waist? Why would Bobby have a dip in the waist? Not at more than two hundred pounds on a five-foot-eight frame. He should be built like a fireplug.

Portland SAR might be looking for Bobby, Alexis realized, her stomach doing another tidal heave, but what she had found wasn't Bobby at all.

YOU JUST HAVE TO LOOK

BEFORE THE WHISTLE SOUNDED, RUBY HAD been moving down the path as silently as a cat.

And like a cat, her attention was sidetracked by all the birds. Dark-eyed juncoes flitted around the forest floor, their white tail feathers flashing. A slightly larger hermit thrush regarded her from a nearby branch, its eyes ringed in white. Ruby's ears picked out the distinctive twitter of a goldfinch from among the pips and trills of other birds. She lifted her head, her eyes following the sound, until she spotted it on a dead limb half broken from a trunk. It was wearing its drab winter plumage with only a ruff of yellow at its throat.

A flash of color farther back caught her attention. Was it? Yes. A pileated woodpecker as big as a raven. Ruby admired its black body, the bold white stripes down the neck, and its flaming red crest. It was stabbing its beak over and over into a dead tree, looking, she knew, for carpenter ants.

Thinking of the birder, she wondered if she herself would ever see a northern spotted owl. Her mom collected owl figurines the way Ruby collected bird sightings. Not only were northern spotted owls nocturnal, but they were also endangered. Just one of the thousands of species at risk of going extinct, thanks mostly to human beings ruining the world.

Suddenly, a whistle broke the stillness. Not a bird's, but something that came from a human throat, forced through a black plastic tube. *Tweet! Tweet! Tweet!* The pattern of three sharp notes was repeated. Someone was in trouble. Without hesitation, Ruby turned back and ran straight toward the sound.

She found Alexis standing just off the trail, pointing at a figure dressed in dark colors lying on the forest floor. It was far too small to be Bobby. And when Ruby pulled off her backpack and fell to her knees beside it, she confirmed that it was a girl. A girl about her own age, with shoulder-length blond hair and green eye shadow painting the one lid she could see. There were no obvious signs of injury, just an ear that bore three piercings.

"Are you all right?" When she was around other people, Ruby was always more comfortable if she could assume a role. This one was easy: First Responder. She leaned into the girl's face, bracing one hand on her shoulder. "Are you all right?" A familiar smell teased Ruby's nose.

In her mind's eye, she saw Jon at the lectern. *Introduce yourself and your level of training. Tell the patient what you are doing and why. Don't make promises you can't keep.* Now she unzipped a small compartment and yanked on a pair of purple vinyl gloves as she said rapidly, "I am Ruby McClure with Portland Search and Rescue. I have first-aid training. May I help you?"

Ruby waited for three seconds, counting in her head. *One jelly bean, two jelly bean, three . . .*

The girl didn't say anything. According to Jon, no response was implied consent. She reached for the girl's wrist. Even through the vinyl glove, it felt cool. Her skin was mottled. Late-stage shock? Ruby reminded herself to ask about nausea and dizziness, confusion and weakness, to check for restlessness or dilated pupils. Rolling her fingers, she found the notch in the wrist and then held her breath. She waited for the pulse in whatever form it might take. Fast and shallow? Slow and irregular?

But there was nothing. Nothing at all.

Footsteps ran up behind her. "Who's that?" Nick shouted. "What's wrong with him?"

"It's a girl." Ruby let the girl's cool wrist slip from her grasp. She gently brushed the choppy blond hair back to check the carotid artery on the side of the neck. After a long moment in which she felt not even the tiniest flicker under her fingertips, Ruby sat back on her heels. "And she's dead."

"Dead?" Nick's voice cracked.

"Call it in, Nick!" Alexis shouted, even though he was only a few feet away from her. It was like neither of them could stop shouting. "You're the one with the radio."

Bending over the girl's body again, Ruby heard the tearing sound of Velcro as Nick fumbled with the rat pack. A squawk, and then, "We found a girl," Nick yelled, not using the proper protocol at all. "A girl on the path you sent us down. And she's dead!"

A calm voice repeated back his words, asked for the

GPS coordinates, and then told them to stay where they were. Ruby heard more Velcro as Nick pulled out the GPS unit, more fumbling, more shouting. Alexis was crying now, big gulping sobs.

But Ruby was too busy looking to pay much attention to all the noise.

What she had at first taken to be a fold in the girl's neck was really a dark red furrow ringing her throat. A ligature mark. The girl had been strangled. Not with bare hands, the way Jack the Ripper was said to have killed his victims, but instead with something narrow slipped around her neck. The Boston Strangler had often used his victim's own stockings, but this girl was dressed in jeans and a hoodie, not a dress. Ruby leaned closer. Shallower scratches ran down both sides of the neck. She lifted the girl's hand again. Two of the nails were broken past the quick.

The girl had tried to save herself. Tried and failed.

"It looks like she was murdered," Ruby said.

"Murdered?" Nick's voice got even louder.

"What do you mean, *murdered*?" Alexis demanded.

"That's a ligature mark." Ruby pointed, but the other two didn't come any closer. "And see those scratches on her neck? She tried to get it loose, but she failed."

Nick swore.

Alexis stared. "How do you know all that?"

"You just have to look," Ruby said. She thought of the limpness of the girl's arm when she had picked up her hand. "I don't think she's been dead long. Not more than an hour or two. Rigor mortis would have set in."

Alexis got the same look on her face that grown-ups sometimes got when Ruby talked about certain subjects.

Nick spun in a circle. "If she hasn't been dead long, doesn't it mean that whoever did this could still be here? Watching us right now?"

CHAPTER 7

TUESDAY

THE NEXT TO DIE

*M*URDERED, ALEXIS THOUGHT. RUBY SAID THE word so calmly, as if she were still talking about one of the birds she had been entranced by earlier.

Alexis couldn't stop staring at the dead girl's face, visible now that Ruby had pushed back her hair. It was all she could focus on. The one eye she could see was nearly closed, and for that Alexis was thankful. She wouldn't think about the thin rim of white on the edge. She wouldn't think about how it felt like, at any moment, the girl might stir and sit up. Maybe not quite human, but still alive.

She had never seen a dead body before. It was hard to believe this was real. It was like she had stepped into a TV show. Maybe one of those guys from *CSI* would show up soon, with sunglasses over his eyes and a gun on his hip, and take charge.

How could a girl—a girl about her own age, with blond hair not that much different from her own—have been turned into a sprawling sack of flesh? That slack mouth would never move again, not even to moan in pain. Not to talk or taste or laugh.

Someone sobbed, grating and harsh. It was only when Alexis sucked in a breath that she realized the sound had come from her.

"What if this guy comes back?" Nick leaned down and snatched up a rock. He raised it above his shoulder, his head whipping from side to side. "He could kill us, too." He was breathing in short, panicked gasps. Hearing him reinforced Alexis's feeling that she had wakened in a nightmare.

Ruby's calm voice set Alexis more on edge than a scream. "Whoever killed this girl did it quickly, even neatly. I don't see any blood. The ground isn't torn up. There are no broken branches or signs of a struggle. But it takes only a few minutes to strangle someone, and after the first ninety seconds or so, the victim is unconscious."

"Is that supposed to make us feel better?" Nick demanded. "Because I don't know about Alexis, but nothing you just said makes me feel better. I don't want to be the next to die."

"You need to look at this logically," Ruby said in a calm voice. "There's no way anyone could kill all three of us without it being noisy and messy, which is completely different from this killer's modus operandi. That's Latin for 'method of operation,' and it's what the police look for in crimes. We're more than likely safe. And, Nick, you should stop moving around and picking things up. You could be destroying evidence."

Evidence. Alexis hadn't thought of that. Even though it bugged her to be lectured, she knew Ruby was right.

"We should all stay right where we are and look for clues," Ruby continued. "But don't touch them."

"She looks about our age." Alexis tried to imagine the girl alive, her face animated. "But I'm pretty sure I've never seen her before."

Nick had finally stilled, even though he hadn't put down the rock. "I know all the girls at Wilson." This didn't surprise Alexis, not with the way Nick ogled any girl who walked by. "She doesn't go there."

"And I don't think she goes to Lincoln," Ruby said. "But that still leaves a bunch of high schools in Portland, plus more in the suburbs."

"I wonder who she is," Alexis said. "And who did this."

Her words made Nick look up and down the trail again.

"And why?" Ruby leaned in to look at the girl's neck again. "Why would someone do this? Sometimes why is the most important question of all."

"What kind of person just kills a girl and dumps her body in the woods?" Nick's breathing had slowed down, but his voice was still too loud, edged with panic.

Ruby pushed the girl's hip experimentally. "It would be a lot for one person to carry up here."

Nick's voice got higher. "You think *two* people did this?" His eyes widened, and his upper lip curled back in horror.

Ruby looked interested. "Maybe. I hadn't thought of that. Or she could have been out here hiking and some-one attacked her."

"She's not wearing boots, though," Alexis pointed out.

Ruby leaned closer to the soles of the girl's shoes. Her legs were curled up so that they rested near her butt. They were dark blue Vans, not hiking boots. "The trail's pretty well maintained. She could have just picked her way around the puddles. And she's got some mud spatters on the backs of her jeans." She squinted, then pointed. "There's a footprint next to her!"

From where she was standing, Alexis could see only a vague outline.

"A million people hike here," Nick said.

"Yeah, but mostly they stay on the trail. And this is right next to her body." Ruby leaned down, putting one hand on the girl's thigh for balance. Alexis's stomach did a slow roll. What was wrong with Ruby that she could treat this poor murdered girl as a convenient place to brace herself? "And this footprint looks fresh," Ruby continued. "Why would there be one right next to the body of a dead girl if it didn't have anything to do with her?"

"I hear something," Nick announced. Like animals at a forest pool scenting a predator, the three of them raised their heads.

Footsteps. Coming fast. A fist closed around Alexis's heart and squeezed. Nick hoisted his rock, but there was nothing nearby for Alexis to defend herself with. Feeling clumsy and slow, she shrugged her SAR backpack onto one arm. Unzipping one of the outside pockets, she managed to find her Leatherman multipurpose tool. The metal was cold and heavy in her hand. She flipped open the blade, which couldn't be more than three inches long, wishing she had Nick's rock. At least you could throw it. The only way you could use the knife was if the killer was already up close and personal. With, say, his hands around your neck.

The footsteps were louder now. "He's coming back," Nick yelled. "He's coming back for us." Throwing down the rock, he turned and ran.

IN THE END, YOU'RE JUST DEAD

A HARSH SOUND CUT THROUGH THE AIR. Alexis's heart stuttered in her chest. Then she identified it as the crackle and squeal of a handheld radio. Which meant that it was probably the good guys coming for them. Not the killer.

Jon burst through the trees, with Mitchell right behind him. "Are you guys okay?" Jon asked, while Mitchell braced his hands on his knees, gasping.

"Yeah, but like Nick said on the radio, we found a girl," Alexis said. "And she's dead." She wondered when it would ever feel real. Jon and Mitchell turned. While no one was looking at her, Alexis folded up her knife and put it away.

"And there's a footprint," Ruby said, pointing. "Not one of the girl's, but fresh."

Skirting the footprint, Jon hurried to Ruby's side, kneeled, and put his fingers to the girl's neck. He was still for a long moment and then shook his head. "You're right. She's dead." He sat back on his heels. "The EMTs should be here any second, but they're not going to have much to do."

"I don't think she's been dead very long," Ruby said. "And there's a ligature mark around her neck. She was strangled with something narrow."

Jon shot Ruby a sideways look.

"We found her, but not Bobby." Alexis's eyes stung. It was all too much.

With his hands still on his knees, Mitchell raised his head. His cheeks were blotched with red. "Team Bravo called it in thirty seconds after Nick reported the body. They found Bobby, and he's okay."

Alexis tried to focus on this one piece of good news. She shifted her stance so that she was no longer looking directly at the dead girl. At the eye that would never again open.

Jon turned to look at her and then swung his head from left to right. Alarm sharpened his voice. "Where's Nick? I thought I told you guys to stick together!"

"He heard you coming and ran away," Ruby said. "He thought you were the killer."

"No I didn't," Nick said, jogging into the little clearing. "I figured it was you guys, but I thought I heard someone coming down the path the other way. I went up to check it out, but I didn't find anyone."

Jon nodded. Alexis wondered if he was buying it.

"I'm sorry you three have to see this," he said. "It's tough to deal with. Even when it's not your first time."

A man and a woman in red jackets and with stethoscopes around their necks sprinted into the clearing. Paramedics. The woman carried a large bag, and the man had a collapsible stretcher on his back. When they saw the dead girl with Jon kneeling next to her, they ran over.

"Don't step on that footprint," Ruby cried out. Just as the man did.

Chris Nagle, the sheriff's deputy, came up the trail a few minutes later. He was accompanied by a Portland cop. After they looked at the dead girl, the two men conferred for a minute and then Chris said, "Alexis, Nick, and—um—is it Ruby?" Ruby nodded, and he continued. "I want the three of you to come over here, but keep to the trail. Or if you're off the trail, go back to it the same way you came in. We need to minimize the destruction of evidence."

"Too late for that," Ruby said, as if the two EMTs weren't right there. She pointed. "That guy stepped on a footprint that was right next to the body."

"That doesn't mean there isn't still more evidence," Chris said patiently. After the three of them carefully made their way back to the men, stepping on rocks and tufts of grass, he said, "This is Officer Ostrom. He's going to ask you some quick questions. We need to preserve the crime scene, so after that you're going to go back down to the parking lot to talk to the homicide detective." Ruby perked up, and even Nick looked interested. Alexis just wanted to get out of there and away from the dead girl as soon as possible.

Officer Ostrom asked who had found the body, if they had seen anyone near it, if they had touched anything. If they knew the girl. Ruby and Nick did most of the talking, often speaking over each other. It was clear pretty early on that none of them knew anything.

Jon led the way back down to the trailhead. Under the trees it had grown dark enough that he told them to put on their headlamps. The temperature seemed to have dropped at least ten degrees. Alexis's teeth were chattering. Three times they passed groups of cops carrying lights, cameras, and other equipment up the trail.

Alexis kept her head down, watching her boots take one step and then another and another. It was nearly hypnotic, the darkness that enfolded them, the bobbing cones of light from their headlamps, the ground that changed subtly with each step but still stayed the same. She tried to focus on what was in front of her. Tried not to think about the girl's eye and how this morning the girl must have put on that green eye shadow and how tonight she was dead. What was the point of doing anything at all if in the end you were just dead?

"It was right there," Ruby complained for the tenth time. "That footprint was probably important evidence."

"Well, it's gone now," Nick said, also for the tenth time. "That EMT guy trampled on it."

Alexis resisted the urge to kick both of them in the butt.

"You guys really shouldn't be talking about what you saw," Jon said. "The detective is going to want to interview you separately. Talking about things can change your memories of what happened."

Once they reached the parking lot, they found the SAR van surrounded by police cars, many of them idling even though they were empty. Another cop got their names, addresses, and phone numbers, telling them they would be questioned soon by a detective and that they shouldn't talk to each other until then. So they waited, alone but together.

Alexis rubbed her hands up and down her crossed arms. She was trembling so hard she felt as if she might fall apart. Someone touched her elbow, and she jumped nearly a foot.

"Are you Alexis?"

It was a guy, but he wasn't wearing a uniform. She nodded, feeling confused. He was too young to be a cop. Too young to be anything except in high school or maybe the first year of college. Nick had been joined by a girl with straight hair, and Ruby was listening to a middle-aged woman wearing a puffy down jacket with the hood pulled up.

"Hi. I'm Bran Dawson." He pushed his dark straight hair out of his eyes and then held out his hand. He was a few inches taller than Alexis. His hand was cool and slightly callused. "I'm with the Trauma Intervention Program."

"That's your job?" Alexis still wasn't following.

"No, I'm a volunteer, like you. TIP likes to call out younger volunteers when the victims are young."

"So they've already figured out who she is?" It was a relief to think that the girl had a name, that she wasn't going to be just Dead Girl Found in Park.

Bran shook his head. "I wasn't talking about the girl who died. I mean you guys."

"But I'm not a victim." Alexis took a step back. "We're not victims. I just found her. That's all."

"Being a victim doesn't just stop with the person who was killed." Bran waved his hand in the direction of Nick and Ruby. "The people who are left behind after something like this—the witnesses, the family, the friends—sometimes they're more affected than anyone else. It just keeps rippling out, and some people can get overlooked. Forgotten."

It still seemed wrong to call herself a victim when there was a real one lying dead in the woods. But Alexis decided not to argue and changed the subject. "So is it Bran like the cereal?"

"Bran like Brandon." He tucked in his lips, looking serious. "But let's get back to you. How are *you* doing?"

Alexis stated the obvious through teeth that danced in her mouth. "I'm really cold."

"Follow me." He walked over to one of the idling cop cars. "Lean against the front fender, and you can get some warmth from the engine."

She did as he suggested. It was a little better. "How come they leave the cop cars on when there's nobody in them?"

"I used to wonder about that, too," Bran said. "But they have tons of electronic equipment—laptops, dash cams, radios—and they all suck up power. If the cops turn off the car, they have to turn off all that equipment or it'll drain the battery. And if they do that, then they can't use it until it reboots." He squinted at her. "Warmer now?"

"A little." But not enough.

"Then we go to plan B." Pulling his keys from his pocket, he ran over to a small brown Honda, opened the trunk, and came back with a gray blanket that he draped over her shoulders.

Gratefully, Alexis pulled it close. Her shivers began to slowly subside.

"So listen, Alexis, I'm here for you," Bran said. "Basically my job is to keep my mouth shut and listen. Really listen. You can say anything you want to me."

"I don't want to talk." If she did, it might make what had happened back there real. And she preferred to think it wasn't.

"Okay. Then I'll just stay here with you." Bran stood absolutely still, not even shifting his weight. He was facing her, but not looking directly in her eyes. He seemed . . . serene. It was not a word Alexis had ever thought would apply to a guy about her own age.

The silence stretched on for a few minutes, but it was even worse than talking. Finally, the words burst out of her. "I keep seeing that dead girl's eye." The green eye shadow on her lid, the rim of white below. "It was almost all the way closed, but not quite, you know? It's like part of me is still standing there in the woods looking at her eye and thinking that at any second it's going to open."

"That sounds scary." His words were even.

"It was like waiting for a zombie to come back to life. I kept feeling like she might twitch and then get up." Alexis looked around the parking lot. "Even now I still feel like I'm in a bad movie. Everything looks too two-dimensional." She gestured with her chin. "Like that's not really a tree. It's something the prop department just wheeled into place and then they hid the wheels behind those ferns."

Bran's smile lifted one side of his mouth. "Feeling unreal, not believing things, that's pretty common after something traumatic happens. It takes a while for things to sink in."

"But I don't want it to be real." Keeping things not real was one of Alexis's skills. "Because reality is awful. Isn't it better for it to feel like a nightmare or a movie?"

"The thing is, Alexis, can you really deal with it if you don't *deal* with it?"

Before she could answer, Alexis heard a choking sound.

It was Nick. He was doubled over, throwing up on his boots.

HIS LITTLE REMEMBRANCE

HE WAS INVINCIBLE.

He was God.

He sat in a parked car a block away, watching as the police scurried around like ants, tiny and useless.

He had walked among them, but they knew him not.

His hands held the power of life and death. Of breath and stillness. Of thought and nothingness.

Lifting them from the steering wheel, he held them out in front of him. In the glow of the streetlight, they were perfectly still. Perfectly controlled.

Today he had taken another life. Taken it and held it close until it dwindled to nothing. Afterward, he had let the girl's empty shell fall on the grass. Then he had leaned down and cut off his little remembrance. *The better to remember you with, my dear.*

Putting his hands back on the steering wheel, he thought about the teenagers he had met, the ones who had asked about a missing man. But only one had captured his attention.

The redhead with milky skin. He had been searching

for such a girl for a long time now. He had seen plenty of brassy reds, hennaed reds, dyed reds, clownlike reds, but this was the real deal. Not from a box or a beauty salon. As pure as nature had intended her.

He had to have her.

ASLEEP FOREVER

RUBY WAITED IMPATIENTLY WHILE THE detective talked to Nick. Meanwhile, a volunteer named Mandy put a blanket around her shoulders and even tried to hug her. Ruby stiffened. She didn't like to be touched by someone who wasn't a relative. Mandy finally stopped trying to get her to talk and fell silent.

The engine of a nearby truck made a ticking sound as it cooled. Every time Ruby breathed, the air slipped inside her lungs like a knife, flat and cold. The detective's car was running, and its headlights cast shadows so sharp they could have been scissored out of black construction paper.

Ruby felt 100 percent alive. Usually at home or school she was playing a role. She observed the people around her, studied their behaviors, and used that knowledge to create a character, like Quiet Chick or Smart Girl, that would allow her to blend in. But tonight she was in her element.

She bounced in place, waiting her turn to be interviewed. Finally the homicide detective beckoned. After shaking his hand, she climbed into the passenger seat. The space between them was filled with three sets of controls, each with lights and buttons. She guessed one controlled the lights and sirens, one a radio, and one the PA system.

Detective Harriman asked her name, address, phone number, and email address. Ruby provided them, even though Officer Ostrom and the other cop had already gotten the same information. She couldn't hold back her own curiosity any longer. "So do you normally do this in an interview room? With one-way glass?" She had a million questions. This was her chance to get the inside scoop on a real investigation.

"This is a field interview," the detective said. "And you're a witness, not a suspect. So this is just how I would normally do it." His features bunched together.

"I like to read about famous crimes," Ruby explained. "The kidnapping of the Lindbergh baby. The Saint Valentine's Day Massacre." She'd picked some of the tamer ones. Not the serial killers. "My mom doesn't like me to watch true crime on TV, but after she goes to bed, I watch it on Netflix on my computer with my earphones."

The detective just grunted. "Why don't you tell me about what happened today."

Ruby took him step by step, from the moment the van had driven into this parking lot to the last look she had given the girl before they left the clearing. For everyone they had encountered on their way up, she provided approximate heights and weights, the color of hair and eyes. "Of course, I'm sure you're aware that eye color can vary depending on lighting conditions."

Detective Harriman's pen had been flying over the

pages of his narrow notebook, but now he shot her another sideways look. "Of course," he agreed. "And you've got quite the eye for detail."

"That's true."

He tilted his head. "So it's like a photographic memory?"

"Not exactly. But it's way better than most people's. Nobody likes to watch TV or go to the movies with me because I can't help noticing all the errors. Like we were watching that movie *Looper* on Netflix last week? And the little boy was playing a game with tiles. When you saw it from his point of view, the tiles were on certain squares, but when you saw it from his mom's, there were fewer tiles and they were in different locations. That's called a continuity error. It happens a lot when they show the same scene from a different perspective. They forget that the character was supposed to have just been out in the rain or that someone was wearing a scarf. Have you ever seen a continuity error?"

He pushed air through his lips, making a *puh* sound. "Okay, Ruby, we're talking about what happened tonight. Not a TV show. Not a movie. And I'm the one who's supposed to be asking questions here. I appreciate that you have a lot of interest in this subject, but I need to stay focused on the task at hand. Not get sidetracked into talking about continuous errors."

"Continuity errors."

"Whatever. My focus is on figuring out who this girl is, why she was killed, and who killed her." His voice didn't sound mad. His face didn't look mad. But even so Ruby thought he might be mad.

"Is this like good cop, bad cop?"

"If you hadn't noticed, there's only one of me." With a sigh, Detective Harriman turned a page in his notebook. "Now tell me again about finding this girl."

So Ruby did. How Alexis had blown her whistle and how Ruby had come running. How she had tried to assist the girl before realizing she was dead.

"So you touched the victim?"

Was he judging her? "I didn't know she was dead. I touched her wrist and neck, but I was wearing gloves. To check for a pulse. It's what we're trained to do." Just remembering made Ruby rub her fingertips together, thinking of the girl's cool skin. "I also brushed her hair out of her face. And later I put my palm on her leg, right below her left knee, when I was trying to see that footprint in the dirt. This was before it got destroyed by the paramedics. All of those I did with gloves on. But before that, I put my palm on her shoulder when I was checking to see if she was conscious. So do you need to swab the inside of my cheek?"

"What?" Detective Harriman's face crinkled up like a crumpled ball of paper.

"For touch DNA," Ruby said patiently. "Because I touched her."

"Everybody watches *CSI*," he said, although he really didn't seem to be saying it to her. "We might be looking for touch DNA, but it's probably not going to be at the spot where you touched her. So you're okay."

"I like knowing things. Like about Locard's exchange principle?" The whole idea was so fascinating that Ruby gave in to the urge to lecture. "Locard figured out that when there is contact between two items, there will always be an exchange. Like walking on a carpet—some of the dirt on the shoes gets left on the carpet, and some of the fibers on the carpet get picked up by the shoes. That's what makes crime scene evidence." She loved Locard's exchange principle because it felt so balanced. So logical. Back in Locard's day, the exchanges had been things you could see with the naked eye. Now the tiniest traces of soil, blood, paint, or even spit could be detected in a lab. "And if you had the ligature," she continued, "you could check it for touch DNA. But the ligature wasn't there."

His eyes narrowed. "How do you know she was strangled with a ligature?"

"No bruises in the shape of fingerprints." Ruby pressed her fingers against her own throat. "There was just a line. So it was made with something thin that made a dent in her skin. But it wasn't too thin, or it would have cut the skin. So not as thin as a wire." She speculated aloud. "An electric cord? A thin rope? A dog leash?"

At the words *dog leash*, Detective Harriman hummed and then made a note. "Lots of people walk their dogs in Forest Park."

"That guy we talked to had two dogs. And he had at least one leash stuffed in his pants pocket. I saw the end of it sticking out. It was red."

Ruby tried to imagine the man they had met coming across the girl and looping the leash around her neck. Yanking it back and tightening it as her hands clawed futilely at her throat.

But if that was what had happened, what had those

dogs been doing? She remembered their muddy paws. But there had been no paw marks or even mud on the front of the girl's jeans.

Ruby knew that when you strangled someone, it usually wasn't about cutting off their access to air by compressing their airway. Instead, death came from squeezing closed the carotids, the two big arteries on either side of the neck. Just thinking about them made Ruby touch her own neck, feel her own regular pulse under her fingertips. Compressing them deprived the brain of blood and the oxygen that the blood carried. In seconds, the girl would have been unconscious. Her head would have flopped forward, as if she had suddenly dropped off to sleep. And then when the killer kept the ligature tight around her neck, she had stayed asleep. Stayed asleep forever.

Detective Harriman's voice interrupted her thoughts. "What else did you notice about the victim?"

"There was mud spatter on the backs of her jeans, so I think she walked up there. I don't think anyone carried her. I think she was killed there."

He made another humming noise as he wrote in his notebook. "Okay. We're almost done. I'm going to need to take a print of the bottoms of your shoes. In case we find any footprints."

Ruby ground her teeth at the memory of how the EMT had destroyed such an important clue.

While the detective took her footprints, Mitchell stood off to one side, waiting for her.

"How are you doing, Ruby?" he asked when she was finished.

"I'm fine." She knew what to say back. "How are you, Mitchell?" Even to her eyes, Mitchell didn't look well. His face was pale and shiny.

"I'm the one who sent three uncertifieds down the trail together." His mouth twisted. "I'm going to get in a lot of trouble."

She tried to reassure him. "No one knew we were going to find a body. Logically, the three of us weren't even going to find Bobby, not in the area where we were going. It was more like a training exercise. You didn't know it would turn real."

"I hope the deputies see it the same way. Since the van already left, they're sending someone out to take us back to the sheriff's office if we want. You drove today, right?"

Ruby nodded, realizing she had been so focused that she hadn't even thought of where her car was or how she would get home.

"We already told your parents you were present when a body was found. But remember that you can't say anything more to them. This is a law-enforcement matter. You can't say it was a girl, you can't say she was murdered, you can't say there was a mark around her neck. Even once it's been released to the media, you can only talk about what's been released. Nothing more. No further details."

Ruby nodded. They had already learned this stuff in training.

"The sheriff's office has called for an evidence search at first light tomorrow. But you don't have to be part of it. It's no problem if you want to opt out. Everyone will understand. After what happened today."

"No. I definitely want to be there."

One side of Mitchell's mouth lifted in a sort of smile. "That's funny. That's just what Alexis and Nick said, too."

CHAPTER 11

TUESDAY

AFTER DARK

A LEXIS WAS EXHAUSTED. THIS DAY JUST kept dragging itself forward, and there was no end in sight. First she had had to wait for her turn to be questioned, had had to watch Nick throw up and then hear him claim he must be getting the flu. Now it seemed like she had been trapped forever in the detective's car as he asked her again about what she had seen, what she remembered, what she guessed. And whenever he finally decided he was done chewing on her and spit her out, she would still have to get home.

"I need to take a print of the bottoms of your shoes," he finally said.

"Why?" Alexis had never gotten that close to the dead girl.

"It's for exclusionary purposes. If we find any more footprints, we want to know if they're yours."

As they both got out of the car, he picked up a slim black folder from the dash. Inside were several long, loose sheets of paper, blank on one side and with a form to be filled out on the other. He flipped back a piece of thin rubber protecting a yellow pad, and then set it on the ground, with the yellow pad and one of the pieces of paper, blank side up, next to each other.

"Okay, step on the yellow pad with your right foot and then put it down on the paper. Make sure you press straight down so the print is nice and clear. That paper costs forty bucks for a hundred sheets."

Alexis did as he asked and then assumed they were done. He set down a second blank piece of paper. "I need the other boot, too."

"But they're the same boots." Still, she was already complying.

"Only when they're brand-new." As the detective spoke, he scribbled her name and the date on the back of the first print she had made. "Once you start walking in them, things happen that make each into one of a kind. You step on a piece of glass or a rock, you wear them down on one side, you scuff your toes—a shoe print can be as unique as a fingerprint." He flipped the kit closed. "Okay. We're done here. Thank you."

Alexis turned to walk down the hill toward the bus stop. She had told Harriman she didn't need a ride home. It would be just her luck for her mom to be outside and for the cop to start asking questions. She had also told Mitchell she didn't need a ride back to the sheriff's office, which was even farther from her house than Forest Park was.

Alexis was so lost in thought that she nearly ran into Bran. She startled backward, her hands flying up in front of her face.

"Whoa, there." He put his hands up. "It's just me."

Her panic left as fast as it had come. "Oh. I thought

you'd left." She'd given him back his blanket earlier. Now she was surprised at how glad she was to see him.

"I just wanted to make sure you had a way to get home again."

"I'm fine. I'll take the bus."

His brow wrinkled. "Can't your parents come get you?"

"No. It's just my mom. And she can't. She's busy tonight." Which was an understatement.

"Won't it take you a long time to get home?"

Alexis shrugged. It would.

"And unless you live near here, you're going to have to transfer downtown, which means you'll be waiting at the bus mall at night. That's not a great place to be after dark."

Unable to think of an answer, she said nothing.

He hesitated. "I'm not supposed to do this. But I'm not letting you take the bus. I'll take you home instead."

"I'm good. Don't worry about me."

He smiled, a crooked grin that slipped right past Alexis's defenses. "But worrying about you is my job."

After a long moment, she nodded. And told herself it was all about not having to take the bus. Not about Bran. She would just make sure he let her out several blocks away from where she really lived.

They walked over to his Honda. Before she could sit down, Bran had to scoop fast food wrappers off the passenger seat and dump them in the back.

"Excuse the mess," he said. "I've been kind of busy lately."

"Don't worry." She plopped into the seat, exhaustion settling over her like a heavy quilt.

When Bran turned his key in the ignition, music blasted out of the speakers. Wincing, he fumbled with the buttons, and the sound abruptly cut out.

"Sorry."

"That's okay. I like Flea Market Parade too."

Alexis gave him an intersection close to her address and added some basic directions, but that filled up only a minute or two. It seemed smarter to ask questions than to answer them. "So why do you volunteer with that group?"

"People do it for a bunch of different reasons. Probably for some of the same reasons you guys volunteer for SAR. Maybe they're interested in law enforcement. Maybe they want to be therapists. Maybe they went through something bad and want to give back."

She noticed he was speaking in generalities. "What about you?"

"Maybe a little bit of all those things." Bran shrugged, his expression opaque. "So anyway, you should know that it's probably going to be a roller coaster for the next few days. You might feel guilty or sad or afraid or maybe all of those things. You might have nightmares or trouble falling asleep or staying asleep. But don't worry, you're not going crazy."

Bran must have caught some flicker on her face, because he stopped his recitation of things he deemed unremarkable.

"What?"

"Nothing. I'm fine. Keep talking."

"The bottom line is that whatever you feel is normal."

Alexis suddenly felt the urge to be honest. "But right now I'm not feeling anything."

"That's normal, too." He shot her a smile. "You might find yourself wanting to learn more about what happened back there, and again, that's normal. But try not to spend too much time chasing down reports. The media can be sensationalistic, and sometimes what they report isn't true at all."

"Okay." His voice was soothing. Every time she blinked, it was harder to open her eyes.

"There are some things you can do to take care of yourself. If you have a favorite band, maybe even Flea Market Parade"—she forced her eyes open and saw him grin at her—"listen to it. If there's any kind of exercise you like, like running or basketball, then spend some time doing that. If you like to draw or paint, do that. I'm not saying paint the dead girl. I'm saying just find a different way to let your emotions out. You might try keeping a journal to record what you're feeling."

It was only because she was tired that Alexis let the next words slip. "Don't worry. I think I'll be okay. I'm pretty good at compartmentalizing." He started to say something, but then she realized where they were. "Hey, this is my corner." It was actually three blocks away. "Thanks."

He pulled to the curb and turned off the car. "Let me walk you to your door."

"No. That's not necessary." The words came out too strong. She took a deep breath and started over. "My mom will have a bunch of questions as it is. If she saw you, she'd want to know all about you. You know. *Moms.*"

She tried to sound like she knew what she was talking about.

Before Bran could say anything more, Alexis had slipped out, opened the back door of his car, and yanked out her backpack. She took a quick look up and down the street, but didn't see her mom. She didn't see anyone.

He rolled down the passenger window and extended his hand, holding a white card. After a moment's hesitation, she took it.

"That's my cell number written on the back. You can call or text me anytime. Whatever you need, I'm here for you. After something like this, a lot of people end up feeling alone. I don't want you to be one of them. So feel free to call or text. Even if it seems silly. Okay?"

Alexis nodded. She had no intention of doing any such thing. She did not need anyone getting closer to her.

OUTSIDE THE BOX

RUBY HAD AN EXCRUCIATING AWARENESS of her own strangeness. No matter how hard she tried, she found it impossible to fit in. Being friends with Alexis had helped. For a while. At least, she thought they had been friends. Now she wasn't sure what had happened, even though she had done her best to be a Supportive Best Friend, a role she had cobbled together from various movies and TV shows. Ruby had treated Alexis to snacks from the vending machine, nodded her head a lot when the other girl spoke, and asked questions to draw her out.

But now Alexis seemed to be avoiding Ruby. Just one in a long line of people who stayed well away from her. It made something inside of her ache, but she didn't know what had gone wrong or what she should do about it.

Some people, teachers mostly, tried to tell Ruby that the way her mind worked was a plus. She had been praised more than once for her ability to "think outside the box." What these boxes were, why they were there, why other people thought they were important, where their borders were, or how you would even know if you were outside them—Ruby had no idea.

And there were so many rules. Rules people didn't even know they had.

Rules Ruby thought often didn't make any sense.

Don't stand too close.

Don't stare.

Take turns.

Don't assume everyone is interested in the same things you are, even if those things are fascinating.

Don't talk about sex.

Don't talk about surgery.

Don't talk about anything that happens in the bathroom.

But the biggest taboo was death.

You weren't supposed to talk about how everyone died. You were supposed to pretend that everyone was going to live forever and ever.

Even her parents were squeamish about the reality of death. And they were doctors! But they were dermatologists, and it had been years since they had had to dissect cadavers. Now they spent their days injecting Botox into rich ladies' foreheads.

Death could come in so many forms. You might get hit by a car or struck by lightning. You might die in your sleep or choke on a Tootsie Pop or develop a tumor that ate you up from the inside. And, most fascinating of all, you might be murdered.

Which was another thing her parents didn't like her to talk about.

And now Ruby had found a real murder victim. Had

actually touched her. She had sat inside a patrol car and talked to a homicide detective.

She had never felt more alive.

When she put her key in the front door, she found her parents in the living room, waiting up for her. Which, Ruby knew, meant something was wrong.

It took her a few minutes to realize what they thought was wrong was Ruby.

As soon as she stepped inside, her mom hurried over with open arms.

"Oh my gosh, are you all right, baby?"

Ruby froze in place to accept the affection. "I'm fine."

Her mom pulled back but kept her hands on Ruby's shoulders. "But they said you guys found a body."

"It all turned out okay, Mom." Although Ruby was still mad about the destroyed footprint. "The EMTs came, and the police, and of course we were with the sheriff's deputy the whole time." The "we" was truthful, if she was referring to all of SAR. Her parents didn't need to know that Chris had been with Team Bravo the whole time. "You didn't need to worry." She took a half step back so that her mom's hands fell away.

"How can I not worry?" Her mom threw a look at her dad, then turned back to Ruby. "You're sixteen years old, and you are out there looking at a murder victim."

Not just looking at her. Touching her. Ruby bit her tongue so she wouldn't say any more.

Her dad finally spoke from where he sat on the love seat. He was still dressed in his running clothes. "We said yes to this because we thought you would be hiking in the woods. Not dealing with homicides."

"And we *were* hiking in the woods," Ruby said. "It was a complete coincidence that we found a body. We were looking for a missing autistic man, and instead someone in our group spotted this body. I could have been bird-watching and had the same thing happen."

"We thought Search and Rescue would be a healthy outlet for your obsessions," her dad said. His arms were crossed, both feet flat on the floor.

"Interests," her mom corrected. She kept reaching out to pat Ruby, and it was all Ruby could do to let her. She was trying to read between the words her dad was saying, but it was hard.

"You like bird-watching, you like the outdoors." Her dad shook his head. "Search and Rescue seemed like a great way for you to be active and to help others."

Mom added, "Maybe make some friends." From the mantelpiece, she took one of her owl figurines and began to stroke it.

"But I have made friends," Ruby said, crossing her fingers behind her back. "Alexis and Nick. And Alexis and I do almost everything together in SAR." She left out the part about their being forced to by the rules, since Ruby and Alexis were the only two uncertified girls.

Her dad pinched the bridge of his nose. "You said you would be looking for people who were lost. We didn't real-ize that extended to dead people and even evidence of crimes." It was true that Ruby had glossed over a few things when she brought home the permission slip for them to sign. "I'm sorry, Ruby, but we're not going to allow you to go out on the search tomorrow."

Ruby's mouth fell open even as her hands balled into

fists. "But it's possible we could find something that would help catch the killer!"

✕ "Watching true crime on TV is one thing, even though it still makes me uncomfortable. But I don't want you exposed to stuff like that in real life."

"I'm not a baby," Ruby said. "You can't hide the world from me. Stuff like murder really happens."

He heaved a sigh. "So does war and torture, but that doesn't mean you need your nose rubbed in it. Finding bodies, looking for evidence, that just reinforces your obsession with the darker side of life."

"But someone has to help people," Ruby said. "Even if it's after they're dead." None of their arguments were logical.

"The person from the sheriff's office said that tomorrow your team will be doing an evidence search where you found that"—Mom's voice caught on the word—"body. You'll miss school to spend eight hours on your hands and knees looking for—what? Drops of blood and cigarette butts and bits of garbage? We don't want you to do anything like that. Especially when you'd miss school." Her mom set the owl back in its place.

"I've got a 3.97 grade point average. It's not like I'm failing."

"I'm sorry, Ruby, but we're not going to allow it."

Everything seemed to go still. "What do you mean?"

Her dad looked at her and then away. "I mean it's over."

"You're going to have to drop out of SAR," her mom said. "We didn't say anything to the sheriff's office because we wanted to discuss it with you first."

"Discuss?" How could her mom even say that with a straight face? "This isn't a discussion. It's an ultimatum."

Her dad shook his head. "Call it whatever you want, but it's our job to make sure you grow up to be a normal human being."

"In case you guys haven't noticed, I'm not normal!"

"Oh, honey," her mom said, and tried to touch her again, but Ruby stepped back and her mom let her hand fall.

"It's settled." Her dad braced his hands on his knees and got to his feet. "You'll go to school tomorrow, not the sheriff's office. And you'll contact SAR and tell them you're going to have to withdraw from the group." He started to go up the stairs, but turned after taking a few steps. "We're only doing this because we love you."

Anger made Ruby rigid, locked her rebuttal in her throat.

"I'm sorry, honey," her mom said in a low voice, and followed him up.

Ruby waited several minutes before she went upstairs. Her parents were wrong to think that Search and Rescue was making her any weirder than she already was. If anything, it gave her a place where she finally fit.

But now it would be gone. And she would be back to being the kind of girl who edited Wikipedia for fun.

OPEN INTO DARKNESS

WHEN ALEXIS PUT HER KEY INTO THE LOCK of the apartment, it was already unlocked. The door swung open into darkness. A shiver ran over her skin. "Mom?" Her voice came out as soft as a sigh.

Silence.

Was her mom asleep? Gone? With someone? Dead?

All of these things were possible.

Anything was possible. Alexis wanted to run. Instead she flipped on the light.

The room showed evidence of her mom's newest obsession. She called them her scrapbooks, but they were more like crazy collages or maybe something there wasn't a word for.

"Hello, my child!"

Alexis turned at the sound of her mother's voice behind her.

Her mom made an elaborate sort of bow, her hands flying into the air like birds, as she crossed one leg in front of the other and gracefully curtsied, keeping her back as straight as a yardstick. She was wearing black pants, a cherry-red sweater buttoned up crookedly, and a new addition: a wine-red velvet shawl that Alexis thought might once have been a curtain. She was barefoot, the bottoms of her feet black with dirt.

Mom was up. Had been since she stopped taking her medication. Alexis wasn't sure how long ago that had been. Two weeks? Three? Despite the light in her eyes, her cheeks were hollow, her eyes sunken.

"Mom. Where were you?"

"I was blessing people in the park."

So it had turned into one of those days. Her mom hadn't been home when Alexis stopped by to get her SAR backpack. The TV had been on, as well as the battered old radio, but at least then the door had been locked. When she was in the grip of one of her delusions, her mom gave little heed to what others thought was normal and necessary.

Take her "blessings." Muttering prayers, her mom would approach anyone. Men walking dogs. Women running. A kid walking to school. A few souls—those too slow or too old or too polite to get away—would end up with her mom marking their foreheads with an invisible cross, using the back of her thick yellow thumbnail.

"Mom. I really wish you wouldn't do that." Why was Alexis even bothering? "You need to get back on your medication."

"But then I can't hear God's voice. He has called me, and I must answer." Her mother's face was serene, but her eyes burned with the urgency of her mission.

"At least don't go out alone at night. It's not safe." The

last few weeks, Alexis had tried to emphasize survival. Life and death.

"God watches over me."

"Can you at least please lock the door when you go out?" The grimy string that should have a key at the bottom was still around her mom's slender neck. She and Alexis shared the same height, the same long hair, the same triangular-shaped face. Only her mom had twenty more years and twenty fewer pounds.

"Have you eaten anything?" Alexis asked, wondering what there was to eat. No answer. She moved into the kitchen. On the counter, there was still half a loaf of bread. "Let me make you some toast." Her mother had followed her in, but she didn't answer. "Come on, you've got to eat something," she said as she slipped two slices into the toaster and pushed the lever. "Please. For me."

"Of course, child. For my one and only Alexis." She reached out and stroked her cheek with the back of her hand. "You are so beautiful."

"Did you even notice I was late?" Alexis said as she went to the front door and locked it. "Did you wonder where I was?"

"God watches over you as well." Her mom nodded as she spoke, agreeing with herself.

"Well, he wasn't watching over this girl we found," Alexis said, and suddenly her head felt liquid. She bit her lip, fighting the tears. The toast popped up. She opened the fridge, but there wasn't any butter or margarine. There wasn't much of anything. Alexis needed to go shopping. Taking one piece of toast, she handed the other to her mom.

"I got sent out with Search and Rescue to look for a guy lost in Forest Park. We didn't find him, but we did find a girl. A dead girl. That's what I was trying to tell you." And suddenly the tears pushed their way through, stinging her nose, burning her eyes. Tears for the dead girl, for herself, for her mother who could someday be a body in the park, if she chose to bless the wrong person. "Somebody murdered her. They strangled her."

And for a moment, her mother was still. Her eyes widened. "You shouldn't have had to see that, baby."

"Oh, Mom." Alexis put her arms around her mother and pulled her close. Her mom was so skinny it felt like she was holding nothing, air and hollow bones. She resisted the urge to lean into her, to be comforted, to be a little girl again, crawling into her mother's lap.

Alexis was dreaming. In her dream, the girl's eye twitched and then flew open. She sat straight up from her bed of leaves and pulled off her own head. It came away with a bloodless pop, like a doll's head.

"Alexis!" The loud whisper was repeated. "Alexis!"

She opened one eye. "What is it?" she mumbled.

"Can we make chocolate chip cookies? I want to make chocolate chip cookies!" Her mom was bouncing on her tiptoes. "With nuts. Walnuts."

"Mom, slow down. Just slow down. I have school tomorrow. You can make cookies if you want, but I need to sleep."

"You're never any fun!"

"I'm sorry." She pulled the pillow over her head.

Her mom snatched it away.

"We need ingredients. I'm going to Safeway."

Alexis sat up. "No. It's the middle of the night." The clock read 2:18. "I don't want you going out this late. The only people up at this time are drunk or"—she stopped herself from saying crazy—"or on drugs."

"But I want to make cookies." Her mom bounced faster and faster. "And I can't unless I go to the store. We don't have the ingredients."

There was no use arguing with her. Alexis was so tired that she had lain down in her clothes, so all she needed to do was push her feet into some shoes and grab the food stamps card and her coat.

The night was cold. Her teeth chattered, while her mother galloped in circles around her and laughed.

"Look at the moon!"

The streets were deserted, except for the occasional car. The neighborhood homeless were all curled up on their makeshift beds, flattened pieces of cardboard laid down in doorways. Alexis couldn't bear to look at them. At times like this, she worried that someday she and her mom might be right next to them.

At Safeway, the automatic door swung open for them. Everything gleamed under the fluorescent lights, all glass and stainless steel. There were only a few shoppers. People who probably never went out in the daylight. Maybe they were vampires. Or zombies, judging by their slow shambling.

Not Mom. She pushed the cart fast down the freezer aisle, then leapt on the back and coasted, giggling. When she saw an old couple watching, she laughed a fake laugh, bright and brittle, as if she wanted to show the other shoppers she was just kidding. Just having fun.

Sometimes Alexis had nightmares that she was with her mom and someone she knew from another part of her life showed up. Someone who thought Alexis was normal. Who didn't know how much work it could be to make people think you were normal.

Alexis got in line. There was only one checker, and three people were ahead of them. Her mom danced from foot to foot.

"This is taking too long," she stage-whispered. "Come on. We'll run out the door and they'll never catch us. We'll run like the wind."

She meant it, too. At this point, her logic was so fractured that she didn't realize how often they were in this very store, that there were cameras on the walls and a security guard roaming, just looking for trouble. In her mom's hopped-up mind, it would be easy-peasy and they would be home in no time flat.

"No, Mom." Alexis kept a tight grip on the cart until it was time to put things on the belt.

As he bagged their order, the clerk shot them a narrowed-eyed look. Alexis had bought sliced turkey, eggs, a head of cabbage, a few apples and oranges. But it was the other ingredients that seemed to cause his disdain. Like they shouldn't be pulling out their food stamp card for butter, chocolate chips, and brown sugar. And walnuts, which cost four dollars for a plastic zippered package that held only a cup. Let him look. Let him judge.

Alexis had seen people buy plenty worse stuff with food stamps—Hot Pockets, Doritos, and bottles of mixer. Homemade cookies didn't seem like too much of a sin.

Back at home, she tried again to sleep while her mom baked. Tried not to dream of the dead girl, lying alone in the woods, the white edge of her eye showing.

DEATH IN
THE WOODS

HER PARENTS MIGHT BELIEVE THAT THEY could make her stop thinking about what happened today, but that was impossible. Long after they were asleep, Ruby sat hunched over her laptop computer, searching for more information.

All the local sites had the basic story of the girl's body being found in Forest Park, and that homicide was suspected. No one had her name or her age or even her cause of death. Only two of the websites mentioned Search and Rescue. If the rule was you could only talk about something that had already been covered by the media, there was little that Ruby was going to be able to say.

Rather than look for other recent crime stories, she went searching for a story she remembered seeing about a month earlier. It took some clicking, but she finally found it.

WOMAN'S BODY FOUND IN WASHINGTON PARK
PORTLAND—Police are investigating the death of a woman whose body was found Tuesday afternoon in

Washington Park, near City of Portland Reservoir No. 4. Reservoir No. 4 is the lower of the two reservoirs in the park. Both are just east of the Washington Park Rose Garden.

According to Sgt. Gene Paulson, spokesman for the Portland Police Bureau, authorities were called to the scene about 2 p.m. by a park ranger who had found the body in a wooded area, just south of the reservoir. A park ranger said the body was not found on one of the park's many established trails but instead along a footpath used by "locals."

The ranger was walking through the area as part of regular patrol duties. The rangers patrol the parks looking for homeless camps and illegal drug activity.

By 4:30 p.m., several police vehicles and the state medical examiner's truck were parked along Jefferson Street, near where it connects with US 26. Homicide detectives were also on hand, as were criminalists from the Forensic Evidence Division.

Then, at about 6 p.m., staff from the medical examiner's office began bringing the woman's body down the hillside. It was covered by a blue tarp and placed in the back of the medical examiner's truck. Investigators also carried evidence bags away from the scene.

The follow-up story had been posted a week later.

POLICE SEEK HELP IN IDENTIFYING DEAD WOMAN

PORTLAND—Police are hoping the public can help them figure out the identity of the woman who was found dead last Tuesday in Washington Park.

A park ranger found the body in a wooded area just off SW Jefferson Street, west of the Vista Bridge. Police said an autopsy showed that the cause of death was strangulation. They also released a description of the woman. They said she was African American, 5'3" tall, 100 pounds, with black short hair worn unstraightened. She had no scars, marks, or tattoos. She was wearing a sweatshirt like the one pictured in the photo at left. Investigators said no recent missing persons cases match the woman's description. They believe she may have been homeless.

Ruby zoomed in on the sweatshirt until it filled up the screen of her laptop. Nobody she knew would have called it a sweatshirt. Instead, it was a hoodie. Black, it had white angel wings drawn on the back, overlaid with pink sparkly curlicues that spelled out the name of a manufacturer of skateboard clothing.

She had seen girls at her school wear that brand of hoodie before. Not because they were skaters, but because their boyfriends were. Sometimes Ruby observed what the other girls wore, trying to make sense of their choices. Like magpies, they collected shiny, eye-catching things. They wore clothes that showed dirt, that were see-through, that wouldn't keep you warm, that had to be hand washed or dry-cleaned, that had flounces and beading and other useless decoration. Sometimes they boasted to each other about the brand, or how much something cost, or dressed in clothes with huge logos that did their talking for them.

Ruby could have happily worn the same thing every day as long as it didn't itch and was more or less clean.

Reading the article, she was certain of one thing. The person who had worn that sweatshirt hadn't been a grown woman, no matter what the police thought. Not a real adult. She knew that determining the age of a body wasn't an exact science. One way was to use X-rays to look at the teeth. If the dead girl had gotten her wisdom teeth in early, they might have decided that she was older than she was.

But while the medical examiner might have made his best guess, he didn't know anything about teenage fashion. Because the person who had worn that sweatshirt probably wasn't any older than twenty.

So the victim was more than likely a teenage girl who had been strangled to death in the woods.

Just like the girl they had found.

ANYTHING GOD DIDN'T PUT THERE

"FEELING OKAY TODAY?" ALEXIS ASKED NICK as they all set down their SAR backpacks a hundred yards from where they had found the girl's body.

Nick felt his face get hot. "My mom's been sick with the stomach flu all week. I must have caught it from her." One minute he had been talking to that counselor girl, Kelsey, the one with teeth like a rabbit, and then suddenly he had been doubled over.

But Nick didn't need trauma counseling, not even from a girl who could be kind of cute if she just closed her mouth. He wasn't some little kid who was going to get all weepy or jump at shadows. So yeah, they had seen a dead body. But there hadn't been any blood.

"You looked pretty upset." Alexis didn't sound like she believed him.

"I'm fine. My dad was in Iraq. He's told me some stuff." Now, where had that come from? Although it wasn't exactly a lie. His dad had been in Iraq, and he would have told Nick stuff if he had lived. Instead Nick had to read about Iraq on the Internet when his mom wasn't home.

"Okay, you two lovebirds," Dimitri called out in his accented English. He was eighteen and one of the certifieds, which meant he had completed the nearly three hundred hours of training. "Please to knock off all those whisperings and get over here for the briefing."

Did everyone think there was something going on between him and Alexis? Nick snuck a quick glance at her, but her face was impassive. *Was* something going on? Maybe she was interested in him. His face felt like it was on fire. He hadn't noticed that everyone was lining up, but now they were all standing with their backs to the crime scene tape that marked out a large rough square about a hundred feet across. Alexis and Nick hurried to join them, standing next to Ruby.

"As most of you already know, a girl's body was found yesterday in this location when we were out conducting a hasty search." Mitchell pointed, and everyone turned. "The body was found roughly in the middle of this square."

As Nick listened, he bounced in place, trying to keep his blood circulating. Per SAR protocol, he was dressed in three layers, top and bottom, starting with long underwear, then a fleece layer, and finally a rainproof layer. Still when he ran his tongue over his front teeth, the inside of his upper lip was disconcertingly cold. He wished he still had his grande mocha, but he had had to gulp it in the van since he wasn't allowed to bring it on-site. Even their lunches would be eaten well away from the search area. They didn't want something of theirs to be erroneously labeled as evidence. In the van, Ruby had gone on and on about the local principle, or something like that.

Before the team had arrived this morning, the cops had marked off the area to be searched for evidence. One end of the square was cut by the trail, and in the middle was the spot where they had found the girl's body. On the way in, they had passed one of the cops who were stationed on both ends of the trail to keep anyone from blundering in.

Detective Harriman stood next to Mitchell. Today he was dressed in a mountain parka and a black floppy nylon hat with a wide brim. When he had first seen it, Nick had decided the hat looked stupid, like something an old man would wear. Now in the slow, drizzly rain, he would have given every dollar in his wallet to buy one. His own wool hat lacked a brim, and even with his jacket hood pulled over his hat and helmet, the rain was still flecking his face.

"Today we will be looking for anything that will help the police solve this crime," Mitchell continued in that super-serious way he had that set Nick's teeth on edge. "It could be as small as a fingernail or a tooth. If you find anything, don't touch it. Instead, call a halt. It's not your responsibility to determine how long it's been there. It's not up to you to decide if it's evidence. Your only job is to find it. Basically, we're looking for anything God didn't put there. Call it and let your team leader decide if the detective needs to check it out."

His gaze swept over the group. People nodded or mumbled in assent.

"And don't get distracted by something far away. Focus on what's in front of you. You don't want to miss something small, like a hyoid bone or drops of blood.

But don't just look down. Sometimes evidence might be higher than your head." Mitchell's coat was unzipped as if he didn't feel the cold. He had a million pouches and holsters suspended from his belt, even more than Detective Harriman.

Toward the far end of the line, someone's teeth were audibly chattering. "You might as well get used to the temp," Mitchell said. "It's not going to get any warmer. Especially not when you're down on your hands and knees." His tone of voice implied this was a good thing, a secret test of their ability and will. "Okay, line up and count off!" He sounded like a drill sergeant.

"One," yelled Ezra, who was standing next to the place where the tape made a corner.

"Two," Dimitri called out. And so on down the line. All of them fast and loud. You were supposed to project when you were looking for someone who was lost, in case it could help them find you. And if the line was spread out, yelling made it possible for either end to still hear each other. But this was an evidence search, which Nick knew from a training weekend meant they would be shoulder-to-shoulder on their hands and knees.

Waiting for his turn to shout, he felt nervous. Which was stupid. It wasn't like you could blow saying your number. It reminded him of calling out numbers to choose teams in grade school. The kind of thing teachers did so that no one felt left out. As if there weren't a million other ways to be excluded.

"Seven," he yelled out. And so on. At the end of the line was a certified named Max. He shouted, "Fourteen!"

Max was wearing the string pack on his back. It

buckled in front, and on the back was a giant roll of string, so much string you could probably fly a kite to the moon. Since there weren't nearly enough people to cover the whole marked-off square in one pass, Max would tie the string to the point where they ended so it could serve as a guideline for the next pass.

"Team forward!" Mitchell called out.

"Team forward," they echoed raggedly. Then they turned, dropped to their knees, and began to crawl slowly under the yellow tape.

"One entering grid!" Ezra called out.

"Two entering grid!" Dimitri yelled a second later. The rule was that you never got ahead of the person on your left.

"Three entering grid!"

Nick's heart started to beat faster. This was the real deal. He could be the one who found something important. Finally it was his turn. "Seven entering grid!"

In a few seconds, they were all under the line and crawling forward. The cold seeped through his leather gloves. He glanced over at Alexis, but her eyes were focused on the ground. Unlike the rest of them, Alexis wasn't wearing padded painter's kneelers. On her hands were regular red fleece gloves, not the leather SAR recommended for evidence work. Her hands and knees must already be wet. He wondered why she hadn't bought better stuff.

Inch by slow inch, they moved forward. Nick's eyes scoured the ground. Dirt, pine needles, pebbles, more dirt, decaying leaves, small plants, slightly bigger plants. At least there weren't any big bushes directly in front of him. The SAR rule was that if you couldn't see through something, you had to go through it, even if that meant tunneling through a blackberry bush. A bad guy might be counting on you not finding his gun because you weren't willing to brave the thorns.

A certified named Jackie was the first to find something. "Team halt!"

The team echoed her. "Team halt!" One by one, everyone straightened up until they were kneeling, all of them looking at Jackie.

Mitchell hurried up behind them. "Who called team halt?"

Jackie, who was a senior, said crisply, "Twelve. Possible evidence." She pointed, but didn't touch. They had been lectured about this several times. If they didn't touch or disturb the evidence, they didn't enter the official chain of custody.

Mitchell leaned over Jackie's shoulder.

"Whatcha got?" Detective Harriman asked, coming up behind him.

Mitchell turned toward him. "A piece of gum, sir."

On the other side of Alexis, Ruby said something about DNA. Nick hadn't thought about it before, but gum must have spit on it.

"Flag it and keep going," Detective Harriman said. Mitchell handed Jackie a small orange plastic flag on a wire, which she poked into the dirt. On their first training weekend, Nick had been a little disappointed to find out that evidence flags looked exactly like survey flags at a construction site. They had been told it was better to flag everything than to stop to collect each item. It made it less likely that they would miss a spot. Only the important finds were worth pulling everyone off the search.

After she finished, Mitchell called out, "Team forward!"

"Team forward!" they answered, a little more in unison. They started crawling again, with Jackie detouring around the gum and the flag.

"Cozy up," Mitchell called. "Shoulder to shoulder. We are aiming for a high POD." POD meant probability of detection.

Alexis was already so close that Nick could hear her breathing. He could even smell her, the scent of something familiar. The press of her shoulder, the sound of her breath, the sweet smell hovering over her, it all made it hard for him to concentrate on the ground in front of him, which basically looked exactly the same as the ground he had already crawled over.

Now that Alexis's shoulder was touching his, he could tell that she was shivering. Well, no wonder. Most of the other kids' waterproof layers were lined coats, but her blue jacket didn't look much thicker than a plastic bag. Her bright yellow rain pants were the kind you could get at any variety store for fifteen dollars.

They came to a tree. Nick was able to maintain his line and go past it, although his shoulder scraped the bark. Since Alexis couldn't maintain her spacing, she had to say, "Eight, out of sequence." That let Nick and Ruby know they had to guide off each other. As soon as they were around the tree, Alexis reclaimed her spot, calling, "Eight, back in sequence."

Now that she was back next to him, there was that smell again. Nick sniffed.

"Why do you keep sniffing?"

"You smell like chocolate chip cookies," he whispered.

Mitchell butted in.

"Stay engaged in the task, people! We need everyone focused on finding evidence. If you're talking, you're not concentrating. If you're talking, you're distracting others. If you're talking, you can't hear commands."

"Sorry," Nick mumbled, and kept his eyes on the dirt and tiny plants and pine needles.

An hour passed and then another. Every five minutes or so, someone would call a halt to flag evidence. They found:

- A cigarette butt.
- Another cigarette butt.
- A third cigarette butt.
- A small piece of black rubber that looked like some kind of stopper.
- A broken piece of flat blue plastic about a half inch long.
- The gold line of cellophane used to open a pack of cigarettes.
- Part of a Snickers bar wrapper.
- A crumpled silver gum wrapper with no gum inside it.
- A little bone, no bigger than the end of Nick's pinky, that surely had to have come from a bird or small animal.

But nothing really cool. No phone, gun, pool of blood, or bullet casing. No old condoms or scraps of fabric. Even Detective Harriman seemed to have lost interest. He no longer came forward to inspect every find.

When Dimitri called a halt for another bit of paper, Nick sat back on his heels and looked behind them. The ground was dotted with dozens of flags.

The search began again. They were just past the point where the girl's body had been found when Nick's eye spied something glinting on the ground right in front of him.

He started to reach for it.

THINGS GO SOUTH

WHAT WAS NICK DOING? RUBY SHOT HER hand past Alexis, who gave a startled gasp, and grabbed his wrist. His forefinger and thumb had been about to close on something a few inches in front of his right knee.

Nick jerked his hand back, and Ruby let go. She saw what he was looking at now. A half dozen strands of blond hair about five inches long.

After Nick called for a halt, Mitchell took one look and then called over Detective Harriman. When he saw it, he made a little grunt. Ruby's gut told her this find was far more important than any of the other bits and pieces they had flagged today. She only wished she had been the one to spot it.

Mitchell and Detective Harriman conferred in low voices. Ruby strained to hear but couldn't make anything out. Then Mitchell clapped his hands. "We're going to break for lunch, people."

Everyone backed out carefully and then went down the trail to where they had left their backpacks. Mitchell and Jon began handing out sandwiches while the others gathered in small clumps and talked.

Instead of joining them, Ruby ducked under the tape and watched the detective.

This morning she had snuck her SAR backpack and outdoor clothes out to the trunk of her car before her parents were awake. Then she had called in sick to the school's attendance office. Her parents got up but didn't say much more to her than good morning. They weren't really morning people, and she guessed that they were just happy she was no longer arguing with them.

After putting her bowl in the dishwasher, she'd picked up her school backpack and called out a good-bye. Instead of driving to school, though, she had gone to the sheriff's office, parked, and hopped into the SAR van.

Ruby had never before defied her parents. But this was her chance to be part of something she had only read about, a real crime scene investigation. Their order had been based on irrational fears. She might be different from other kids, but being part of SAR was good for her. She was socializing with her peers, the way her parents always advocated. And because of the clues they were discovering, SAR might actually help catch a killer.

She watched with interest as Detective Harriman took a series of photos. The first ones showed the larger scene from outside the crime scene tape. Next he ducked under the tape and took medium-range shots that included the spot where the girl's body had been. Then he took close-ups of the pieces of hair, using a flash to show every detail.

For the last set of photos, Detective Harriman laid down a ruler. Finally, he pulled on gloves, carefully gathered the hair, and slid it into a small, clear evidence envelope. That envelope went into a slightly bigger manila envelope, which went into his coat pocket.

When he was done, he wove around the other evidence flags and ducked under the crime scene tape. Ruby followed him. They both grabbed sandwiches.

He walked off as he started to unwrap his sandwich. When he realized she was still following, he turned around. "Yes?"

"Another girl was found murdered in Portland a month ago. Strangled in Washington Park. Did you know that?" In case he didn't, Ruby had a printout of the article in her coat pocket.

His eyes narrowed. "It's not like we have that many homicides. And I heard that wasn't a girl. That was a woman. An adult."

"Have you identified her yet?"

"No." He didn't offer anything more.

"But look at the hoodie she was wearing." Ruby pulled the color printout from her pocket and unfolded it. "No adult would wear that. Girls at my school wear that brand all the time. It's something skaters wear. Skaters and their girlfriends. And when you consider the angel wings and all that pink and sparkles, you've got something that no woman would wear."

"Uh-huh," the detective said. He was nodding rapidly, which Ruby had learned meant either that he felt it was his turn to speak or that he was bored. Or maybe both.

"So that makes two. Two homeless girls strangled in Portland. Maybe there's a serial killer. And a lot of serial killers strangle their victims."

Detective Harriman sighed. "The truth is that a lot of murder victims are homeless people. They panhandle, so they're constantly interacting with strangers. It's pretty common for them to sleep outside, which means anyone can walk right up to them and they won't even know until it's too late. They're vulnerable, mobile, and nobody asks too many questions if one of them just disappears. But none of that matters, Ruby, because we've already got an ID on the girl you guys found yesterday. And she's most definitely not homeless. She goes to school right here in Portland."

"What school? What's her name?"

"That information hasn't been released yet. We're still notifying relatives." His gaze sharpened. "And remember, you can't talk about what you learn here. What happens in SAR stays in SAR."

"Don't worry. I already know that. But I still think you need to consider whether it's a serial killer."

"Look—it's Ruby, isn't it?"

She nodded.

"So, Ruby, I'm tired. Late last night I had to go tell these parents that their baby girl was dead. Do you know how hard that is? Now I just want to eat my lunch without having to make conversation and then I want to go back out there with you guys and find the clues that will help me catch this girl's killer. That's all I want. I don't want to talk about whether it's a serial killer, because it's not. We have a homeless black woman and a rich white high school girl. Serial killers have types. They don't just go around killing anyone."

"They were both strangled." Ruby reiterated the obvious.

"So? Strangulation is perfect if you don't want to make much noise, if you don't want to attract attention." He held out one of his big hands, all hairy knuckles, and flexed it. The other was still wrapped around half a sandwich. "It doesn't even require any special tools. And just because someone gets strangled doesn't mean a serial killer did it. A guy might go to rob someone, or there's a physical altercation, and things go south. When he doesn't have access to a weapon, he has to use the only weapons he's got. His hands."

"But was the other girl also strangled with a ligature? The newspaper didn't say."

"Okay, Ruby, that's it." Detective Harriman waved his free hand. "Get out of here and let me eat my sandwich in peace."

They spent another three hours searching, finding two dozen more small bits of trash but nothing Ruby considered of any significance. By the time they finished, her knees were aching and her chilled hands had lost some fine motor skills.

When they got back to the lot where the van was parked, a reporter for the *Oregonian* was waiting. Detective Harriman didn't allow him to ask questions, but he did let him take a photograph of them walking down the trail, and he gave their names. Mitchell said it would be good publicity for the unit.

Ruby realized it also meant she had to figure out something before her parents picked up tomorrow's paper from the driveway.

HIDDEN

THE GIRL COWERED ON HER KNEES, ARMS tied behind her back. Her blue eyes were wide over the white gag that separated her full red lips. Her black hair tumbled over her shoulders.

Nick's drawing was only in pencil, but in his head, he still saw the colors. He was seated in the far back corner of the meeting space at the sheriff's office, his free hand shielding his paper. Doodling helped him to focus on what was being said, allowed him to sit still, but he had found that most adults didn't understand. Not just the act of drawing, but his choice of subject matter. One of his teachers had even claimed his drawings were "disturbing." Which was ridiculous.

Tonight they were covering urban searches. Jon said, "Usually in an urban search, we're looking for either very young children or old people with Alzheimer's." He clicked on the next PowerPoint slide, which showed a guy in a yellow helmet carrying a sleeping toddler. "In some ways it's easier because the navigational landmarks in an urban area are pretty clear. I mean, we've got street signs. But urban searches are also harder, because the subject may not want to be found or may be being purposely hidden by an abductor."

Nick started a new drawing, one with him in it. A slightly idealized version of him. Some of the other guys in class looked more like men, with muscled chests and thick arms. Nick was wearing a T-shirt he'd gotten in ninth grade, and he still didn't fill it all the way out. In the drawing, he gave himself strong arms to hold the girl, her head hanging back, her breasts jutting out like twin mountains.

At the break, he tucked the paper in the back of his binder, then gathered with the others around the lemonade and tray of rubbery snickerdoodles from Safeway that the sheriff's office provided.

"Can I give you guys a ride home tonight?" Ruby asked Alexis. She was using a napkin to pick up the carton of lemonade. Nick had noticed she didn't seem to like to touch things.

"Sure," Nick said, who far preferred Ruby's car to the bus. But why was Ruby offering both of them a ride? Alexis lived on the other side of the river. Not that he would mind riding with her.

"Oh, that's okay." Alexis was already starting to move away. "I'll just take the bus."

"Actually, it's important." The lemonade dripped on the table when Ruby set it down. Instead of wiping it up with the napkin, she swiped at it with the cuff of her sweater. "There's something I need to talk to both of you about." She leaned closer and whispered, "In private.

About the girl." By the time she reached the word *girl*, Ruby was only mouthing it.

Alexis's eyes widened and then she nodded.

"Is this really your car, Ruby?" Alexis asked after she opened the passenger door of the black Scion, illuminating the interior.

Nick remembered how surprised he felt when he had first gotten a ride with Ruby. How could someone who seemed to have issues with germs have such a filthy car? The interior was filled with loose papers covered with scribbled notes, thoughts, and diagrams. Some of the papers were actually unopened mail. Bowls and plates sprinkled with bread crumbs and wilted bits of lettuce were stacked on the back seat and scattered across the front passenger floor next to cups with dried orange juice or old coffee congealed on the bottom.

"Sorry," Ruby said absently as Nick clambered into the back seat, bulldozing everything over to the other side. Alexis picked up a garbage-stuffed Burger King bag from the front passenger seat and then looked around uncertainly. "What should I do with this?"

Ruby tossed it over her shoulder and said, "So the dead girl's name was Miranda Wyatt, and she lived in the West Hills."

"How do you know that?" Nick asked. The West Hills was one of Portland's most expensive neighborhoods.

"I overheard Chris telling Jon."

He guessed it hadn't been much of an accident. Ruby was like a cat, always quiet, creeping around the edges, slipping unseen through shadows.

"And I've been thinking," she continued. "We're the ones who found her. We're the ones who talked to all those people that day. Maybe we saw something that could help find the killer."

"That's why Harriman interviewed us," Nick said. "But we *didn't* see anything."

"Sometimes things that don't seem like clues turn out to be," Ruby said. "Don't you want to help figure out who did it?"

"Aren't we supposed to not talk about it?" Alexis asked.

"That was only talking to outsiders," Ruby said. "Not people in SAR. I think whoever killed Miranda Wyatt might be a serial killer."

A thrill raced from the soles of Nick's feet to the top of his head.

"A serial killer." Alexis didn't look impressed. "This isn't a movie, Ruby."

"There are serial killers in real life, Alexis, not just in movies," Ruby said with more than a trace of impatience in her voice. "The FBI estimates that *right now* there are somewhere between thirty-five and fifty serial killers active in the U.S. *alone*. And that girl we found, Miranda, she isn't the first dead girl found in a Portland park." She pulled a printout from her pocket and put it on the center console, then turned on the overhead light. "Check this out."

Nick and Alexis bent over the short article. Ruby stabbed her finger at the photo of the hoodie the body had been found in.

"They're saying that she was an adult, but look at that hoodie. I've seen that brand at my high school a lot. And that particular one is all pink and glittery on the back. No adult would wear that. I tried to tell Detective Harriman, but he wouldn't listen. He thinks the two deaths aren't connected because the victims are too different: one's a white rich girl, and one's a homeless black woman."

Alexis thought, but didn't say, that an adult like her mom might still wear that hoodie.

"But they were both strangled," Nick pointed out.

"According to him, a lot of women are strangled, but that doesn't mean it's a serial killer. But the thing is, some serial killers strangle their victims because they like having the ultimate power. It's literally in their hands as to whether the victim lives or dies."

At Ruby's words, Alexis shivered and then drew her coat tighter around her. Nick wished that she were sitting in the back seat with him so he could casually drape his arm over her shoulder.

Ruby continued, "The FBI says there are two kinds of serial killers: organized and disorganized. Disorganized ones are messy and don't have a plan. This guy is probably organized, which means he's smart, plans his crimes, and lures his victims as opposed to forcing them. Ted Bundy used to put a fake cast on his arm and ask his victims to help him carry his books. Or organized serial killers will target people who willingly go with strangers, like prostitutes. They follow their own crimes in the media. And—this is really weird—it's pretty common that after they're caught, people who know them say they are kind and would never hurt anyone."

"How could that happen?" Alexis asked. "How could they be like two different people?"

"A lot of serial killers are sociopaths. They're born without empathy. They don't understand that other people have feelings, too. It's like they're born broken. Most of the time they try to fit in, but if you've got something they want, you're about as important to them as the paper wrapper a hamburger comes in."

THE SOUND OF HER LAST BREATH

THE GIRL WAS SITTING WITH HER BACK against the kitchen door of a restaurant that had gone out of business. Her knees were drawn up to her chest, and she was resting her face on them, so that all he could see was the back of her head and the nape of her neck. At her feet was a piece of cardboard that read ANYTHING HELPS. Next to it was a paper cup from Starbucks with a few coins on the bottom.

It was her hair that had attracted his attention. Cut in a bob that showed off the long lines of her neck, it was black, thick, and straight. He imagined burying his nose right behind her ear. How he would inhale as he listened to the sound of her last breath.

A longing filled him. He turned and looked to the left and then to the right. No one out for a walk. Not even any cars passing by. It would be so very easy—

"Oh!" She lifted her head so fast that it thumped on the door behind her. Wincing, she looked at him suspiciously from eyes set off by black bangs cut square across.

She couldn't have been out on the streets long, not

with how neatly trimmed those bangs still were. She was even younger than he first thought when he had seen her from across the intersection. Fourteen, fifteen? How did a girl like this survive on the streets? Where did she eat? Was this really where she slept?

"Sorry if I startled you. I'm with Hope for the Homeless." The group didn't exist, but he doubted she would be Googling it anytime soon. "Would you like a pair of gloves?" With his own gloved hands, he opened the white plastic Target bag. He had bought dozens of them for a dollar apiece. They came in a rainbow of colors, plus black-and-white stripes.

Her face opened up. "Oh, thank you. My hands get so cold." She reached for a turquoise pair and slid the left one on. They were linked with a plastic tie, which she bit in half with straight white teeth.

"You're awfully young to be out here on your own," he said. "It's not safe." She didn't know the half of it.

She straightened her spine. "I can take care of myself."

"But what if someone tried to hurt you? This street is deserted."

"See that?" She pointed above her head. "That's a camera."

It *was*. There was even a small sign just behind her head that he only now noticed. "Property under surveillance."

As he looked at the camera with his face tipped back, every feature surely clearly visible, he felt sick. How many times had his image been caught by a camera affixed to a building? Had someone been watching him while he had been watching these girls?

"I always make sure I sleep under cameras to protect myself." The girl lifted her chin. "This lady I met told me about it. She said that one time a guy lit her blanket on fire while she was sleeping, but it was all caught on camera."

He thought but didn't say that the camera hadn't stopped the woman's blanket from being set on fire.

Since his face had already been captured by the camera, he looked at it more closely. Who had put it there? There were no government buildings on this block, and it wasn't angled to capture traffic. It must be privately owned, just meant to deter burglars. The more he examined it, the more it looked like an empty black camera-shaped box. No wires led to it, and it wasn't moving.

"But what if something bad did happen?" he asked. "Do you have a phone so you could call someone?"

She shook her head and dropped her gaze.

"Would you like one?" With his gloved hand, he took the phone out of his pocket and offered it to her.

She pulled off one of the gloves he had just given her and ran her finger across it, making a happy sound as it blinked to life. It was a prepaid cell phone, bought for cash at Walmart. And not just the cheapest phone, the kind you could only make phone calls with and that was all. No, with this phone you could go on the Web. You could listen to music. You could download apps.

And you would never notice that another hidden app was already loaded on it.

"It comes with a month of prepaid service."

Her mouth thinned down to a line. "What do you want for it?"

She was wary now. Even at fourteen or so and not long on the streets, she knew there were trades. Knew that nothing was free.

"I just want you to think about calling your family. Or seeing if there is another place you can go. It's not good to be out here by yourself."

If she took it, he would know exactly what she did with it. Who she called. Where she was.

Suddenly she thrust it back at him. "I can't take this."

"Why not?" This was only the second time he had tried giving a homeless girl a phone. The first time it had disappeared into the girl's pocket so fast it had been like a conjuring trick.

"It's too valuable. I wouldn't feel right."

"But we want to help girls like you." The "we," he thought, made it seem more legitimate.

"Thank you, but no." She continued to hold it out until he took it.

Time for his backup plan. "I'm afraid I'm all out of food coupons, toothbrushes, and socks," he said, as if he had ever had those things to begin with. "I still have lip balm. Would you like one?" He was confident she would say yes. She would still feel awkward about refusing the phone. Lip gloss was on the same level as cheap synthetic gloves, a gift small enough that it didn't demand anything in return.

"Oh, okay." She nodded. "Sure."

He dropped the black tube into her upturned palm.

And it really was lip balm. At least the top third of an inch was. It weighed just four grams more than a real ChapStick, but inside the tube was a GPS unit that would continuously broadcast its location until the tiny battery that powered it ran out. He had sealed it with a piece of cellophane heated with a heat gun.

She uncapped the balm and ran it across her mouth, then offered him a shy smile with newly glossy lips. "Thank you!"

"You're welcome," he said. "And have a good night. Stay safe."

He didn't allow himself to grin until he had turned around and was walking away.

YOU'RE ONE OF THEM NOW

ALEXIS CLIMBED THE STAIRS TO THEIR apartment, so tired she could barely lift her feet. When she had signed up for Search and Rescue, she had thought it would be easy. Maybe even boring. Just putting one foot in front of the other. Helping the occasional lost hiker. Not learning how to read topo maps. Not finding dead people. Not flagging tiny white scattered bones. Even if Ruby was certain they had belonged to an animal.

When Alexis opened the door, her mom was in the living room, a game of solitaire spread out on the coffee table. The TV was showing a *Seinfeld* rerun, the sound turned down to a murmur. This morning Alexis had made her mom a peanut butter and jelly sandwich. It sat untouched next to her cards, the bread beginning to curl at the edges.

"Why didn't you eat your sandwich, Mom?"

"Why were you so eager for me to eat it?" Her mom's stare challenged her. "Did you crush up some of those pills and mix them in?"

It was probably a good idea, like hiding a cat's pill

in a ball of tuna fish. "No, I didn't," Alexis answered honestly.

"You'd tell me the same even if you were lying." Maybe her mom's brain was working better than Alexis thought.

"Well, I'm not." She moved toward the kitchen. "Here, I'll make you a new sandwich, and you can watch while I do it."

"How do I know you didn't just stir something into the peanut butter earlier?"

Off her meds, her mom could get like this, sliding into paranoia. Alexis didn't have the energy to deal with her. "Fine. Then don't eat. I'm going to take a shower."

She had carried Bran's card with her all day, occasionally reaching into her jeans pocket to rub the ball of her thumb over the top edge. Now before she could think too hard about it, she pulled it and her cell phone out, then typed his number into a text program.

In the message line, Alexis typed, Hey B—Spent all day looking for evidence. Long day. Alexis.

Looking at the clock at the top of the screen, she decided she would give him five minutes. If he didn't respond, she would flip her phone closed and go take a shower.

While she waited, she decided to see if she could find out more about the dead girl, Miranda Wyatt. Was Ruby right? Had Miranda been the victim of a serial killer? Someone who might kill again?

But before Alexis could even go on Facebook, her phone chimed.

Bran: Hey A, how are you doing? Did you sleep OK? B.

Her hands were sweating. She wiped them on her pants legs before she typed her answer.

Alexis: A few bad dreams. Up in the middle of night making choc chip cookies.

As she hit the return key, she thought about how every word she had typed was true, but not the whole truth.

Bran: Good choice! Let me know if you ever want to share.

What was she doing? Bran would want her to share more than chocolate chip cookies. He'd want to know more about her life. And it was safer if she kept herself to herself.

Alexis: I'll let you know. Just wanted to update you. G2G.

A fine tremor washed over her as she hit the END button. Trying not to think too much about what she had just done, Alexis slipped the old white MacBook from underneath the bed. It was her connection to the outside world. Her cell phone only allowed her to go on the company's website, which just had links for sports, weather, and news, all of them excruciatingly slow, especially when you had to pay for every minute you used. Not having a cell phone that could go on the regular Internet was nearly as weird as saying you didn't have a TV. Which sometimes they didn't, depending on whether her mom had been gripped by one of her rages. Luckily everyone was swapping out their heavy TVs for flat screens, so in the last few years it had become easy to pick up a replacement for ten bucks or less. Their apartment came with basic cable offering a handful of stations. When you were living on your mom's disability check and food stamps, you didn't have a lot of choices.

The MacBook was six years old, a gift from one of her babysitting clients, and you had to know just where to touch the trackpad. Still, with it and the neighbor's borrowed Wi-Fi, Alexis could go on Facebook, Tumblr, and Pinterest, and could even research school papers.

On Facebook, she clicked around until she found Miranda. In her profile photo, she was sitting in what looked like a backyard at dusk. On her forehead, a circlet of white flowers. With a grin, she looked off to one side, her cigarette trailing silvery smoke in the night air.

Luckily, Miranda and Alexis had two friends in common, which meant Alexis could go deeper into her page. Of course, "friends" was a loose word on Facebook. In real life, no one had 579 friends. Not close ones, anyway. Despite her couple hundred friends on Facebook, Alexis didn't have even one close friend in real life.

Today, Miranda's friends had left a string of messages.

Mir everyone loves you so much.

We are all in shock. We just can't believe you won't come back to us with that crazy grin.

Mir—our hearts are broken without you.

I loved you, Miranda. Should have told you that when you could hear me. But it's still true.

Yesterday morning, Miranda's friends had thought they had all the time in the world to tell her things. Yesterday, Miranda had been just one of thousands of high school girls in Portland. Now no one could talk to her and everyone would talk about her.

Alexis clicked around on Miranda's Facebook page. She had attended Alder Grove, a private alternative school that Alexis knew was for kids who were on the verge of dropping out and whose parents had lots of money.

Then she clicked on the button for Miranda's photos, and her mouth fell open. Photo after photo of Miranda looking wasted, hanging out with people who looked sketch, in places that looked trashed, with broken furniture and tagged walls.

In the first photo, she was outside, just as she was in her profile picture. Only this time she posed in a black bra and panties, arms crossed just above her pierced belly button, flashing deuces. She was a pretty girl, but not so pretty standing amid a pile of black trash bags on a street someplace, her feet bare, her grin stupid, her eyes dead.

Miranda was clearly a risk taker. Maybe Ruby was right. Maybe she had done something to bring herself to the attention of a serial killer. Alexis closed her laptop and was still mulling it over as she walked through the living room on her way to take a shower.

When she saw Alexis, her mom leaned closer and whispered, "What are they saying?" Then she pasted on an enormous fake smile and said, "Don't worry. There's no reason to be afraid."

Alexis's stomach dropped. "What are you talking about?"

"Shh!" Her mom's eyes darted to the TV set, where Jerry was sitting in the coffee shop talking to Elaine, Kramer, and George. The sound was turned too low to hear more than murmurs. "Them. The watchers. What are they saying?"

"Mom, they're on TV. It's not real. That show's, like, twenty years old. The actors are saying whatever the script told them to say two decades ago." Reality and her mom had clearly parted company. "And they're not watching us."

Her mom shook her head, still keeping her voice low. "They are. You just can't see it. They're sneaky, the watchers. They like to keep you off guard." She stood up. "I can't stay here. Not while they're watching our every move."

"Mom, they're not watching." Alexis went over to the TV set and pushed the power button until the picture blinked off. "There. Now they're gone. Okay?"

"You just can't see them." Her mom's eyes narrowed. "They're still there. They're still watching."

With a grunt, Alexis heaved the TV so that it faced the wall. "Okay. Now they can't see anything. Just the wall."

"They've gotten to you." Her mom's mouth turned down at the corners. Her eyes were full of betrayal. "You're one of them now."

She grabbed her mom's arm, thin as a stick under her sweater. "Mom, it's okay, I'm not one of them. Mom!"

"Get away from me!" Her mom scooted backward. "I know who you are!" Her eyes were panicky, twitching like a scared rabbit's. Alexis grabbed her again, but her mom wrenched free and ran for the door.

By the time Alexis made it to the hall, the door was slamming shut at the bottom of the stairs.

WHEN SHE WAS FINALLY STILL

THE *OREGONIAN* LAY WAITING FOR HIM ON THE otherwise empty old oak table. He set the plate down in front of it. The cobalt blue Fiestaware held three over-easy eggs, lightly salted and peppered. He'd bought the cage-free eggs at the farmers' market. Because they came from a variety of breeds, each shell had been a different color, one creamy white, one brick colored, and one blue-green. Inside, they were all the same, with yolks an orange-yellow to rival a summer sun.

Picking up his fork, he flipped past news from the Middle East, past flooding, past celebrities, past football. He cared about none of it. But on the front page of the Metro section he found what he was looking for. A story about the girl. Her full name was Miranda Wyatt.

Setting the side of his fork against a yolk, he slowly increased the pressure until it dimpled and then broke and ran, coating the tines with sticky yellow liquid. Eating in quick bites, he read the article.

Until now, he had known only the girl's first name. But she was his; she would always be his. Her name was ultimately unimportant. He still had the data he had gathered about her. Unlike many of the homeless girls he had met, she hadn't spent her nights downtown, but in the West Hills near an upscale grocery store. She had told him about digging through the store's Dumpsters to find something to eat, and then bedding down behind them on pieces of cardboard.

The section of her blond hair that he had cut away with his pocketknife was now in his office, tied with a green velvet ribbon. He could touch it anytime he wanted to remember her brief struggle against the inevitable. He could look at the photo he had snapped of her when she was finally still.

In the newspaper's photo, which appeared to have come from a high school yearbook, the girl looked so different. Her hair was tucked behind her ears, not hanging in her eyes. The only piercings he could see were in her ears.

And now she was gone, and it was time to move on to something new. Something different.

Someone different.

The article was short, taking up far fewer column inches than the two photos—one of the girl, the other of a search team—that accompanied it. He remembered when newspapers had been substantial. Thick with pages, with words, with ideas. Now the paper was about as weighty as a *Star* magazine. You could even be illiterate and still enjoy the pictures.

He skimmed through the details of her life, frowning a little. She was well liked, she was survived by her parents and an older brother, and she went to a high school whose name he had never heard.

A high school in Portland. That gave him pause. Miranda had said she was a runaway, but the paper said she was a student at this school, which was described as "alternative." Maybe it catered to homeless students.

Had she been lying to him? Or were her parents lying to the newspaper?

Or did it really matter? He had begun to think that his little experiment was too narrow. That he needed to broaden it.

He was about to turn the page when a milk-pale face among the line of searchers caught his attention. It was that girl who had captivated him. He read the caption. Her name was Ruby McClure. Ruby. What a perfect name. She was like a rare and precious jewel. The photo was black-and-white, so her hair looked undistinguished, but he remembered its rich red color.

He slipped his plate into the dishwasher and then went into his office. So far, he had distributed eight GPS trackers, retrieving one after it was no longer needed. Each tracker reported its location every fifteen minutes. Once he sent them out into the world, he could look up the trackers online, either at home or on his phone.

On his computer, he checked the current location of all his girls. It looked something like an air traffic control screen, only the blinking green dots represented homeless girls in downtown Portland. If he hovered over a dot, it would tell him the number he had assigned to the girl carrying it.

It would be easy enough to buy Ruby's home address online, but how could he find a way to track her? If he followed her and engineered a meeting, she would certainly have her own phone. And he didn't think she would take lip balm from him. Even if she had been homeless, he didn't think she was the type who would take anything at all. So he would have to find a way to hide it in her belongings without her noticing.

And suddenly it came to him.

From a drawer, he took out the jeweler's loupe and put it to his right eye. He picked up a pair of tweezers. From a jumble of objects he kept in another drawer—cigarette lighters, watches, belt buckles—he selected what looked like a thumb drive.

Humming "Greensleeves," he set to work.

Alas, my love, you do me wrong,
To cast me off discourteously
For I have loved you well and long,
Delighting in your company.

ALL OF THEM GONE NOW

"ME AND THE SAR TEAM ARE IN THE *OREGONIAN* today," Nick told his mom and Kyle. He sat down at the dining room table and reached for the orange box of Wheaties. "They took a picture of us yesterday after we completed the evidence search. For that *murder* investigation." Nick might be three years younger than his brother, but here he was, playing an integral part in something as serious as a murder investigation.

Neither his mom nor his brother were exactly morning people. His mom nodded as she leaned against the kitchen counter and drank her coffee. She was a cashier at Fred Meyer, a regional supermarket chain. Kyle shrugged, his eyes at half-mast. He was slumped over his cereal bowl. One hand propped up his head, and the other held his phone. He was checking his texts while his Wheaties turned to mush. In the evenings, he took classes at Portland Community College, and during the day he sorted packages for UPS. Sometimes on weekends Nick and Kyle played first-person shooter video games together, but other than that, he was completely off Kyle's radar.

"So?" Kyle said. "Who reads the paper anymore?"

Unfortunately, he had a point. This morning, Nick had gone looking online for the picture. But he didn't know anyone who actually read a physical copy of the paper, or even checked it out on the Web. Certainly not anyone his own age.

"The photo's online, too." It sounded lame. Everything was online, so nothing was special. Their photo was competing against videos of impossibly cute kittens and crazy skateboarding tricks.

After looking at the *Oregonian* website, Nick had tried going to Miranda's Facebook page, but because of the way she set her privacy settings, all he'd been able to see was her profile photo. It had been so weird to look at her smiling face, her cigarette, and her circlet of flowers, and to think that all of them were gone now. The flowers compost, the cigarette crushed, the girl dead.

Kyle started typing a message with one thumb. With a sigh, Nick added milk to his cereal.

The coffee maker hissed as his mom pulled the pot free while more fresh coffee was still trickling in. She dumped the few ounces into her mug and slid the pot back. She never ate breakfast, but always insisted that they did.

"Are you sure you should be doing this?" She pressed her lips together. "You're only sixteen. When I signed the permission slip, I thought it was going to be about rescuing lost people in the woods."

Nick realized that he had better recalibrate, and fast.

There was no point in trying to make Kyle think he was cool. In attempting to make him realize that, even though Nick couldn't remember his dad, he was the one who was going to follow in his footsteps. Nothing he did had ever impressed his older brother or would ever impress him in the future. If Nick said that yesterday he had fought off a serial killer and saved a beautiful girl, Kyle would just shrug and go on scrolling through his phone. On the flip side, if his mom got too freaked out about SAR, she could pull him out.

"There are kids in SAR younger than me." A couple of the guys were fifteen, although neither of them had turned out for the search yesterday. "It was fine. To be honest, it was kind of boring. Spending hours on your hands and knees, staring at the ground, flagging little pieces of trash that the wind blew in. Next time I hope we get called out to help someone."

Her lips folded in on themselves. "I hope so, too. Because spending a bunch of time where that poor girl died doesn't seem healthy." More coffee burbled into the pot, but she left it alone, so he knew she was serious.

"I think it's helping my ADHD," Nick improvised. "It's, like, teaching me to concentrate."

Kyle shot him a sharp look. Nick wondered if he was actually paying more attention than he was letting on. It might still be worthwhile to try to get him interested. Just not when their mom was around.

"I don't understand why they don't have real cops doing something like that." She finally noticed the new coffee and poured it into her mug, then added another splash of milk.

"They did have a detective there to check out what we found. But if they put fourteen cops on their hands and knees for a day, then they wouldn't be out on the street writing tickets or catching bad guys. And we don't cost anything."

"Still, you had to miss school to do it. If your grades drop, you're going to be out of there." She tossed back the rest of her coffee and put her mug in the dishwasher.

"I know, Mom. You said that already. Don't worry." This hadn't gone at all the way Nick had imagined it would. All it had gotten him was a shrug and a lecture. He couldn't wait to get to school. He started shoveling in his cereal.

At school, all anyone could talk about was Jericho Jones, the best quarterback Wilson High had ever seen. Only last night Jericho had been driving around with Robbie Bellflower, who had dropped out last year. Robbie had pulled a gun and robbed some guy at a bus stop. Both Robbie and Jericho had been arrested, and Jericho was probably going to be suspended as well, maybe even expelled. Apparently it didn't really matter that the gun had turned out to be an Airsoft that shot only BBs, not bullets.

Still, Nick tried to work the evidence search into conversation at every opportunity. Before the bell rang for first period, he turned around and talked to Kylie Milani, a blond girl who sat behind him and who was railing about the unfairness of Jericho's fate.

Nick saw an in. "They don't think it was a gun that killed that girl in Forest Park, but we had to keep an eye out for one anyway yesterday when we were searching for crime scene evidence." He tried to hew to SAR's rules. "Our orders were to look for anything God didn't put there. I found something that was so important that they pulled everyone off the field so the homicide detective could check it out. I can't say what it was, though."

He closed his mouth meaningfully and waited for her to ask. But it was like he was invisible.

"Without Jericho, our team is going to suck," Kylie said. "And it wasn't even a real gun."

As he was finishing lunch, Nick saw Sasha Madigan carrying her tray to the garbage and hurried so they arrived at the same time.

"I don't know if you saw the paper today, but they've identified that dead girl whose body we found in Forest Park the day before yesterday. Her name's Miranda Wyatt. She went to Alder Grove Academy. I helped the cops with the evidence search yesterday."

Sasha was staring at him, balancing a pink wad of gum between her front teeth. He had imagined kissing her so often, but a lot of times she didn't even answer his texts.

"The homicide detective thinks that I might have found a key piece of evidence."

Nick waited for Sasha to ask him what he had found. Maybe he might even tell, after swearing her to secrecy.

Instead she said, "Wait. You were crawling over where her body was? Like, on the exact same spot?"

"Yes. The same spot." Well, close enough.

Her nose wrinkled. "Gross! Like, did it smell or anything?"

"What? No. I don't think she had been dead very long when we found her." He wasn't even supposed to say that, but Sasha still didn't seem interested.

When he was in biology, a voice came over the intercom. "Nick Walker, Nick Walker, please report to the office."

From the back of the room came a few catcalls. A guy's voice singsonged, "Nick's in trouble!"

Could he be in trouble? As he got to his feet, he reviewed everything he had said so far today. He had basically stuck to what the *Oregonian* had printed. He hadn't given anything away. Not really. But what if someone had called the sheriff's office?

In the office, two girls were sitting on the bench informally known as the "bench of doom" because it was where you waited to talk to the vice principal. Josie Karl had eyes outlined in black eyeliner a half inch thick. She looked exotic, like some cross between a lemur and a girl. And Becca Berry was wearing a skirt so short she really shouldn't be sitting down in it.

Not that Nick was complaining.

"I'm Nick Walker," he told the office lady, Mrs. Weissig. With over a thousand students, the only people whose names she really knew were kids like Josie and Becca. Kids who spent a lot of time on the bench of doom.

She pressed her lips together, and he forgot all about Becca's skirt. "Nick, a Detective Harriman just called. He wants you to come down to police headquarters." Her face was stern.

His heart seized. *Oh, crap.* When would he learn to think before he spoke? Was he going to get kicked out of

SAR? Would this screw up his joining when he turned eighteen?

Her next words interrupted his internal monologue. "The detective said they have a suspect they want you to look at." She nodded meaningfully.

He realized that she was impressed. Mrs. Weissig, who had seen everything. Twice.

It was like a gift. Nick raised his voice. "So you're saying the Portland police want me to come down and identify a murder suspect."

She nodded, her double chins wobbling. "That's what they said. Except for the murder part."

Her correction didn't matter. Because Josie and Becca were already whispering.

Nick Walker. Key witness in a murder investigation.

IN A DARKENED ROOM

RUBY FOUND A PARKING SPOT ONLY TWO blocks from the Portland Police Bureau's Central Precinct. Her heart was beating fast. If they wanted her to look at a suspect, then it must be one of the people they had met on the trail.

Her parents still didn't know she had taken part in the evidence search. This morning she had set the alarm for early and smuggled the newspaper to her room where she had hidden it. Last night, Ruby had played the Good Student, a role she had found her parents particularly liked. She had claimed to be studying at the library and had even come home with a stack of books she had checked out before class.

As she walked toward the police station, Ruby ran through what she knew about lineups. There were two kinds: photo and live. And there were two ways to conduct each kind: simultaneous and sequential. Sequential was the most accurate. In a simultaneous lineup, human error could creep in. A witness viewing a group of potential suspects might pick the one who looked most like the person who had done it. But "most like" was not the same as "the one." The Innocence Project had freed hundreds of wrongfully convicted prisoners, and most of them had been sent to prison by witnesses who had misidentified an innocent person as the bad guy.

On TV, it was always a live lineup, probably because that was more interesting visually. Ruby felt a little shivery as she imagined herself in a darkened room, peering through one-way glass, watching a group of men shamble in and then turn and face her.

"Got any money?" a guy asked, startling her. He was only a few feet away, dressed in a dark hoodie and jeans. His cheeks were hollow, and his backpack was covered with layers of patches. Even though he was clearly a street person, Ruby thought he was her age, at most a year or two older.

"No," she said. "Sorry." And bit her lip so she wouldn't add that he smelled. Her mom was always reminding her not to make any personal observations that might be perceived as negative. The only exception was if the person could remedy the situation immediately. But the reek hovering over this guy like a cloud seemed sort of permanent.

Central Precinct's lobby was a soaring circular space, empty except for a directory set in green granite. The floor was made of alternating squares of pink and white marble laid on the diagonal. Uniformed cops walked quickly past Ruby, their steps echoing. On either side of the room, stairs curved upward in perfect symmetry, flanked by shining silver handrails. They looked like they belonged in some movie from the thirties, the kind Ruby's grandma liked to watch. As if two matching sets of chorus girls dressed in feathers and spangles would soon come high-stepping down either side. But the stairs were empty.

Posted on the wall was a notice that visitors had to check in at the front desk. She finally found it in a narrow, low-ceilinged hallway tucked behind the lobby. On the other side of a thick sheet of Plexiglas sat three clerks. Ruby leaned close to one of the round silver grilles. Next to her, a Hispanic man pressed a torn scrap of paper against the glass and muttered, "I need to talk to this guy."

"I have an appointment to see Detective Harriman." Her breath was coming faster. Was the man next to her an informant? A wanted man?

After checking a list, the woman took a pen from behind her ear. Ruby was momentarily distracted, thinking about an old episode of *30 Rock* she had watched the night before. In one shot, Kenneth had had a pen behind his ear. But when the camera showed him from the front, the pen hadn't been there.

The clerk slid the pen and a red and white badge under the Plexiglas. It read VISITOR with a line underneath for a name. Ruby printed her name and then stuck the badge to the front of her jacket. She pushed back the pen, but didn't know what to do with the backing she had peeled off the tag. The clerk's blank expression offered no clue. Would it be rude to give it back? Finally she folded it up and put it in her coat pocket. The microphone buzzed and snapped when the clerk pressed a button and spoke to her in a monotone. "Go to the end of the hall and wait by the elevator doors." Ruby did as she was told.

The doors slid open, and Detective Harriman stepped

out, holding a file folder. He shook her hand, his face unsmiling. His hand was warm and dry, and she hoped her own didn't provide too much of a contrast.

"I have some photos I'd like you to look at," he said as he pressed the button for the elevator so that it opened again. "To see if you recognize any of the people as being in Forest Park on Tuesday."

No live lineup. Ruby felt a pinch of disappointment. Oh well. It was enough to just be here. "Is there a particular person you're looking for?" she asked. "We saw several."

"Just tell me if you recognize anyone in the photos." He sighed. "That's all you need to do."

After they stepped off the elevator, he walked her past fabric-walled cubicles that buzzed with ringing phones and dozens of conversations. They went into an interview room. There wasn't much to see—blank walls, a square table, and two chairs that didn't match. One was on wheels and one not. She guessed he would take the one on wheels, and he did. The wheels meant that he could change the space between himself and a suspect in a second, rolling up close to coax a confession in a near whisper.

Ruby could feel her pulse in her ears. How many people had confessed in this room? What dark deeds had been revealed? She looked around. "Where's the one-way mirror?"

Detective Harriman sighed again. "Those are all gone, except for on TV shows. These days it's just a video feed that can be watched on a monitor." He laid the file folder between them. "Now, see if you recognize any of these people as someone you saw on the trail on Tuesday. I'm going to show them to you one at a time. They aren't in any order. With each one, I want you to tell me if you recognize the person. And it's possible that none of the photos I'm about to show you belongs to anyone you saw. You need to be sure. It's just as important to protect the innocent as it is to find the guilty."

He opened the file folder. Inside was a stack of photos facedown. He turned over the first. A white man, about thirty, with a round face. "Do you recognize this man?"

Ruby had never seen him before. She shook her head and then said no, in case this was being recorded.

The detective turned the photo back over and picked up the next one. Superficially this man bore some resemblance to the first guy—white, around thirty, a full face.

So that was the type of person they were looking for. Ruby ran through the people they had met while they were looking for Bobby. The guy running with his dogs had been a little older and thinner. The bird-watcher was much older and had white hair and a beard. The homeless guy had darker skin and dreads. The guy on the mountain bike had been younger and had a little goatee. Of course, it was easy enough to change the appearance of your hair or for a man to shave, but your age and the shape of your face would be harder to alter. Still, Ruby thought they must suspect the man with the duffel bag.

He showed her two more photos, neither of which she recognized. Even though she was half expecting it, Ruby still sucked in her breath when Detective Harriman turned over the fifth photo.

He froze, looking at her.

"It's him. I saw him on the trail. The guy with the blue duffel bag. He told us he hadn't seen anybody."

"You're sure it was him?"

"Of course I am. I remember those little eyes and the way the bridge of his nose looked fat, like it had been broken once."

Detective Harriman grunted. "I still have to show you the rest. We just have to be sure."

"You can, but there's no point. I'm certain."

"It's part of the procedure, Ruby." He turned over one photo and then another.

She said no twice and then he was finished. "How about the other people we saw?" she asked. "Have you contacted them, too?"

"We talked to the bird-watcher and the mountain biker. But so far we haven't been able to locate either the guy running with his dogs or the homeless man."

"What about the ones you did talk to? Did they see anyone?"

He let out a huff. "Ruby. I can't really talk about that."

Was she going to be the sole witness who could put the guy with the duffel bag on the scene? Surely he was having the others view the photo lineup. But what would they say? "Are you having Nick and Alexis come in, too?"

Detective Harriman said, "Right now I'm interested in what you saw, Ruby. Not them."

"It's just that I've read people are much better at picking out faces of people who are within their own race. Only all the people we saw that day were white except the homeless guy. And I think Nick is half African American. That might affect his perception."

"Ruby, I appreciate that you are a crime buff." There was a dissonance between his words and the expression on his face. "But let me remind you that this is my investigation."

"Okay, okay." She nodded rapidly. "What about this guy's shoes?"

"Shoes?"

"What did the soles of his shoes look like?"

"We didn't recover any clear prints made by anyone other than people in SAR and the first responders. That's why we printed you guys that night. For exclusionary purposes."

"If I saw that footprint again, the one that was next to the body, I could tell you if it was the same one."

"I don't think that will be necessary, Ruby." Detective Harriman leaned back, lacing his fingers across his belly. "You may have already given us everything we need."

IF THEY KNEW THE TRUTH

LATE AFTERNOON, AND HE WAS BORED. People treated him as if he didn't matter. As if they didn't even see him. Their ignorance grated. If they knew the truth of who he was, of what he had become, the stupid smirks would be wiped from their faces. Their mouths would fall open. And then they would tremble in fear.

At moments like these, when everyone tried to make him feel powerless, he returned again and again to the memory of his first time, playing it out in slow motion. He let the moments slip through his mind like pearls on a string, each one precious and distinct.

He had met her downtown. She told him she was hungry, and the hollows in her cheeks underlined the truth of that. At a nearby McDonald's, he bought her a hamburger, fries, and some kind of abomination called a McFlurry, but suggested they go elsewhere to eat.

They went to the park. It was a perfect Indian summer afternoon, the turning leaves, shades of yellow and red, silhouetted against the bright blue sky.

The food was gone in just a few bites. She sucked the

salt and ketchup from her fingers, but her fingernails were still rimmed with dirt. Her eyes were shadowed. She told him stories, some true, some maybe not so true. Her life, it seemed, was a mess. She had run away from her family in San Diego, spent time with a cousin in Vancouver, and then found it necessary to move on to Portland.

In turn, he shared a little about himself. About his interests. Tried to explain them to her.

But while she listened to him—or pretended to listen—her face, which had been so animated when she spoke about herself, about her problems, grew slack and expressionless. And then when he had tried to interest her further, she had been careless. Had nearly broken something that was precious to him.

He had only meant to reprimand her, but things had escalated and she had gotten upset. Then he had simply sought to stop her shrieking. But she had fought him, forced his hand.

He remembered how her eyes had widened. How her hands had clawed at her slender throat. How her mouth had opened and closed, the cords standing out in her neck. And how she had finally, finally stilled. Then he had laid her down and regarded his handiwork.

She had given him a present, without even meaning to. A wonderful surprise.

Her death had showed him the gift of life. A gift which was within his power to give.

Or to take away.

STILL GONE

ALEXIS STARTED UP ON ONE ELBOW, HER pulse racing. She had left the lamp on in the living room, and now she stared at the empty rectangle of light framed by her doorway. Had she heard the lock turning in the door?

"Mom?" she called, then held her breath so she could hear the answer. Her alarm clock read 2:38.

No footsteps, no shadows. Not even the sound of another person's breath.

It must have been another tenant. Or even a dream. Her mom was still gone. Slowly, Alexis lowered her head to the pillow.

It took her a long time to get back to sleep, and when she woke, nothing had changed. It had been forty-eight hours since her mom raced out the door.

Alexis was going to have to do something. But what? If she went to the police, they would ask questions, and everything would spiral downward from there. Her mom was always saying it was just the two of them, that "they" wanted to put her away, wanted to split them up. For a long time, Alexis had thought that when her mom talked about being put away, she meant jail. Only as she got older did she realize her mom meant a mental hospital.

Was that where her mom was? But then wouldn't they have done something about Alexis, too? Taken her off to foster care when they realized she was all on her own?

Where could her mom have gone? Alexis checked the basement laundry room, but it was empty. Next she stopped by Perk Up, the coffee shop down the block, where the owner sometimes paid her mom a few dollars to sweep the floor or wash dishes.

"Sorry, honey, I haven't seen her," Mara said. She rubbed her eyes, looking as tired as Alexis felt. Mara was not just Perk Up's owner but the sole employee, selling coffee in a city where there was a café on every corner.

Alexis scribbled her number on a napkin. "Could you call and leave a message if you do see her?"

"Of course." From the day-old basket, Mara took a cinnamon roll wrapped in plastic and pressed it into her hand. "Is your mom okay?"

"I hope so," Alexis said. "She just got upset about something."

In the park two blocks from their house, she peered behind bushes and under evergreens for places her mom might have nested. All she found were empty beer bottles, fast food wrappers, and two discarded needles.

Back in the apartment, she unearthed a phone book and called the closest hospital, Emanuel. "Um, do you have a patient named Tanya Frost?"

"She's not in our listing."

Alexis tried to keep her voice from shaking. "Well, do you have any unidentified female patients who have been brought in during the last few days?"

"No." The operator's voice changed. "Honey, is everything okay?"

Alexis hung up.

Presumably there was also a morgue she could call, but again, that seemed like it would result in too many questions.

Plus, wouldn't she know in her heart if her own mother were dead?

Maybe she was going about things in the wrong way. If official people had her mom, they would have contacted her. She needed to look in places that weren't so official. Her mom wasn't homeless, but when she was off her meds, she certainly seemed to be. The best place to be crazy in Portland was downtown. If her mom wouldn't come to Alexis, then maybe Alexis would have to go to her.

On the bus downtown, Alexis made herself eat the cinnamon roll. It was hard to swallow, but she told herself that was because it was a day old.

The bus let her off a few blocks from the main library, which opened at ten. While she waited for the doors to be unlocked, she covertly surveyed the people waiting on the stone steps. A mom with two little kids. A gray-haired old lady with a stack of books. But it was the others Alexis focused on. The girl in front of her wore her hair in two high pigtails, and one of her sneakers flapped at the toe. The guy next to her had black pants hacked off at mid-shin. His red socks didn't match in length or hue. Both he and Pigtail Girl smelled. It wasn't just BO but the smell of clothes that had layers of dirt and spilled food ground into them.

How long would it be before Alexis was homeless herself?

A figure appeared on the far side of the library's doors. Everyone shuffled forward. As soon as the door was unlocked, Alexis raced to nab one of the computers.

On Facebook, Ruby had sent her a message with a link to a story on KATU.com about the guy with the duffel bag. His name was Jay Adams, and he had been charged with Miranda's murder. Alexis looked at his booking photo for a long time. His eyes were small and set deeply in his full face. His mouth was a line. She wondered what it would feel like to turn your face to the camera, to know this photo of you would always be associated with a horrific crime.

A law enforcement officer who wasn't authorized to speak about the case said that Adams had been cultivating a marijuana patch deep in Forest Park. From that site as well as Adams's home, police have reportedly recovered a .45-caliber handgun, two knives, and 56 marijuana plants. The source said Adams had cut down several trees to increase the amount of sunlight and had also run irrigation lines from a nearby creek.

The source, who is close to the investigation, said the working hypothesis is that Miranda Wyatt had stumbled across the grow and that Adams strangled her to keep her quiet.

That big blue duffel bag he had been carrying must have been filled with pot. Alexis remembered how he had shifted nervously while he spoke to them. What would he have done if they had asked about the bag?

She printed out the article, which had Miranda's photo at the bottom. Later, when her mom was normal again, she could show it to her. Because her mom would be okay, right? She always was. Eventually.

Next Alexis printed out a photo of her mom from one of her Facebook albums. All their real photos, the ones printed on actual glossy photo paper, had been purged from their apartment last year when her mom had been off her meds and decided that they were graven images, something the Lord apparently didn't approve of.

After signing off the computer, Alexis went to get her printouts from the central printer. You weren't allowed to sleep at the library, but that wasn't stopping people from trying, propping their heads on their fists, or laying a book or magazine over their tilted-back faces. After scanning the room to make sure her mom wasn't among them, Alexis slipped both printouts into her backpack and walked out the front doors. More homeless had gathered on the stairs and the concrete benches, turning their faces up to the weak late fall sun.

So many of the homeless were her age. Sleeping curled in a doorway, sporting piercings or holding a cardboard sign, or cuddling a kitten or a puppy or a full-grown dog on their laps. But never a cat. Where did the cats go?

Alexis shivered. She was wearing a hat, gloves, and a coat. Her mom had run out without any of those things.

She walked for blocks and blocks, looking at dozens

of homeless people, without catching a glimpse of her mom. She was going to have to start asking.

A man in a black hoodie, dirty jeans, and heavy boots leaned against the wall of a building across from Pioneer Square. His cardboard sign read I WANT YOUR $. His bony face was unsmiling, as if you had better pay him or else.

Most people were ignoring him. A few took the long way around.

Alexis walked right up to him. "I'm looking for this woman." She shrugged her backpack off one shoulder. "Last time I saw her, she wasn't wearing shoes."

He scowled at her. His eyebrow and lip were pierced with silver. Still, he took the printout she handed him. "Yeah, I've seen her around."

"You have?" Excitement jolted up her spine.

"Yeah. Freaking oogle." He sneered at her. "So is that your game, too? Come in from the West Hills and do a little slumming? Pretend to be homeless and ruin it for the people who really are?"

"What are you talking about? I'm just looking for my mom."

"That's your mom?" He looked back down at the printout, equal parts puzzled and repulsed. "That chick's not old enough to be anyone's mom."

Alexis took the piece of paper back.

She had shown him not the photo of her mom but the photo of Miranda Wyatt.

CHAPTER 25

SATURDAY

ALL THE CHOICES
IN THE WORLD

THE HOMELESS GUY WAS STARING AT HER, confused. From her backpack, Alexis took the print-out with her mom's photo. "This is who I really meant," she said. "This is my mom."

He squinted at the photo, then shrugged and leaned back against the wall. "At least that one looks old enough to be your mom. But her I haven't seen."

This wasn't getting her anywhere. But what he had said nagged at her. Why had he recognized Miranda? Alexis took out the news story again.

"How do you know this girl? And what did you say she was?"

"I don't *know* her." He looked at the headline. "Or maybe I should say I didn't know her. Because it looks like she's dead. But I've seen her around. She's one of those stupid oogles."

"What's an oogle?"

"Oogles are posers. They like to hang out and pretend they're part of the 'homeless scene.'" He waved his hand at a man sleeping underneath a bench, a tattooed girl curled up on the pavement, an older couple with a dog and a coffee cup containing coins that the woman rattled hopefully. "Like *this* is a scene. Like this is a choice, like it's some party you can drop by and then leave when you get tired of it. But for some stupid reason, oogles like to playact."

"Wait. You're saying this girl liked to pretend she was homeless?" Alexis thought of the other dead girl in the article Ruby had shown them. That girl had been homeless.

"Some rich kids get off on that. They come around, and they try to talk the talk, walk the walk, the entire act. They'll get a piece of cardboard and make a sign and spange."

"Spange?" Alexis echoed.

"Beg for money. You know"—he changed his voice to a whine—" 'Got any spare change?' When really they're all from Beaverton or the West Hills, and they're not homeless. They're just bored. And because they're bored, they're the ones who get drunk and stupid, they're the ones who vandalize stuff or tag, and we're the ones who get blamed for it."

Alexis nodded slowly. Now Miranda's Facebook photos made sense. She had been slumming, partying with the homeless. Or, perhaps more likely, with other kids who liked to pretend they didn't have parents or homework, that they didn't even have a home.

"They try to act like they're just like us. But at night, they're not sleeping in a shelter or behind a Dumpster. They're not going to bed hungry. Because they have nice warm beds and nice warm meals waiting for them at home." He spit out the word *home* like it was an obscenity.

"It's like sitting in a wheelchair because you think it will be fun and then hopping out when you get tired of it. Well, we don't get to hop out. Do you think I like living like this? I don't have any choice, but those stupid kids have all the choices in the world."

"But my mom's not an oogle." She dared to say the truth out loud. "She's mentally ill."

He didn't seem to find this remarkable. "Out here, who's not?"

Even though she couldn't really spare it, Alexis gave him a dollar before she moved on to ask more people if they had seen her mother. No one had. Lunchtime came and went. All she had had to eat today was the stale cinnamon roll. But she never stopped scanning the people she saw, looking for that familiar tall, lean form. And not finding it.

Finally Alexis gave up and decided to go home. Maybe her mother would be there. Or there'd be a phone message. Or even a letter. Still scanning faces, she walked to the bus mall. She had spent enough time waiting here to know that many of the people milling about under the shelters had no intention of riding the bus. Some were homeless. Some simply liked having a place to sit out of the rain. And panhandlers and proselytizers were drawn to a captive audience who didn't want to walk away in case that was the moment the bus came.

Alexis had long ago developed a stare that said, *Don't mess with me.* It went well with a set jaw and narrowed eyes.

But in the mirror this morning, her eyes had been haunted, her face pale, her mouth trembling. And she

135

couldn't deploy her don't-mess-with-me blank stare because she was still looking for a glimpse of her mom.

Her eye was drawn to a man and a teenage girl who were arguing in low voices. The guy was nondescript—especially when Alexis was just looking at the back of his head—but the girl was a hot mess, with her greasy black hair, dirty clothes, and the tiny blue star tattoos swirling on one cheek.

He yelled at her, then grabbed her wrist, but she twisted free and ran past Alexis. It all happened so fast that she didn't know if she was the only one who had seen him grab her.

The man took a few steps to follow the girl, then stopped, shaking his head in frustration. He turned and walked away.

Alexis was frozen in place, had been since she saw his face. She knew this guy, even though he was dressed in a dark sweater and jeans and didn't have any dogs with him.

It was the guy they had seen running along the trail the day they found the dead girl.

STEP ONE

ONE POINT THREE MILES, THE TRAIL
marker said. George Hines could do that, easy.
After all, he had done it seven years ago. It was just a little
day hike. Step one in getting back in shape.

It wasn't long before he was audibly huffing. The
trail—not paved, just a rutted track in the dirt, winding
between evergreens—was much steeper than he
remembered.

Fifteen minutes after he began, George's eyes were
focused only on his blue Nikes as he concentrated on
putting one foot in front of the other. He couldn't turn
back around. What kind of man was he if he couldn't
even hike 1.3 miles?

But seven years ago, George had been fifty pounds
lighter. Seven years ago, he hadn't yet taken up smoking
again. And seven years ago, he had begun this hike at
eight in the morning in June, not three in the afternoon
in early November.

Some time later, he lifted his head. And blinked. It
was getting dark. He turned in a slow circle. Pools of

shadow lay under the trees. He had forgotten about day-light savings time, about how night suddenly crowded in.

George had no idea how close he was to the end of the trail or, for that matter, to his car. He checked his backpack as if a flashlight might appear, but all he had was his lighter, his smokes, and a bottle of water. He uncapped the water and took a long drink, turning a bit to look at the darkening sky, then put the bottle away with a sigh. He was going to have to head back for his car. Maybe he would still tell Doreen he had done the whole route.

He started back the way he had come. After a half dozen steps, he stopped. Was this the right way?

George looked one way and then the other. They both looked exactly the same. Trees, a faint path, deepening shadows. He tried holding up his lighter, but the tiny flame just revealed how black it all was now.

Something cold landed on his cheek, but it was gone by the time he raised his fingers to it. Then another flecked his nose. In order to see the numbers on his digital watch, he had to press the button on the side to light it—5:22. He was lost. In the woods. In the dark. And it was starting to snow.

Pulling his cell phone from his pocket, George called home. "Doreen, it's me."

"Where are you?" She sounded both anxious and relieved. "I thought you would be home by now."

"The truth is, I'm a little lost."

The 9-1-1 dispatcher told George to stay where he was, that help was on its way. She asked what he was wearing.

Jeans, a T-shirt, a light jacket. Now that he was no longer moving and the sun had completely slipped below the horizon, he was cold. So cold. In response to her questions about supplies, he told her that he didn't have a pocketknife, a first aid kit, extra clothing, rain gear, food, or matches. He didn't have a flashlight or a headlamp or a compass. And he was no longer even sure that he was actually on the trail.

George was no longer sure about anything, except it suddenly seemed possible he might die.

IN GOOD SPIRITS

Search in Columbia Gorge. Lost hiker. Meet time 1830.

Nick's mom was making a big pot of chili when he showed her the text. "Can I borrow the car?" He knew she wouldn't be going out. She never did. She said one man had been enough for her. On Fridays and Saturdays, she stayed home and watched old movies on TV.

She turned with a frown toward the window. "But it's already dark out."

"People get lost at night, too, Mom. In fact, that's probably why this guy got lost. Once it gets dark, people tend to panic."

"I don't know." She bit her lip. "Are you sure it's safe?"

"Of course it's safe. It will be a big group. Almost everyone else has done dozens of searches."

Kyle came into the kitchen. He lifted the wooden spoon to his lips and took a taste, something their mom would never let Nick get away with. "Let him go, Mom," he said, to Nick's surprise. "He's not a baby. And it's not like you're using the car."

She grabbed back the spoon. "I notice you're free enough handing out my car, but you would never let your brother use yours." Kyle had his own car, a 1996 GTI.

"Because I need mine tonight, and you don't need yours. Besides, what if this guy dies because Nick's not there to save him? You don't want that on your conscience."

Nick couldn't tell if Kyle was mocking him. He sure hoped not.

Deputy Chris Nagle drove them out to the Columbia Gorge. Jon was riding shotgun, half turned in his seat so he could address the people in the van, a mix of Alpha and Beta teams, of certifieds and uncertifieds. "Look, everyone, I know that right now you might be feeling tired of SAR and burned out, what with the hasty search on Tuesday and the evidence search yesterday, plus class last night, plus today's search. That's a lot. I'll be the first to admit that this has been a tough week. Even so, we need to be careful that we don't end up with short tempers, or compromising our judgment, or not paying attention. All those things are easy traps to fall into, so we'll have to watch for them."

Everyone nodded, with different degrees of enthusiasm. Nick thought Ruby and Mitchell looked a little too eager, while Alexis seemed distracted.

Then Jon told them more about the lost subject, George Hines. George had no map, compass, flashlight, food, extra clothing, knife, first aid kit, signaling device, or emergency blanket.

Next to Nick, Ruby gave her head a disapproving shake at each deficiency.

On the plus side, George Hines had no known medical conditions, unless you counted him being overweight and a smoker. His supplies consisted of a lighter, a cell phone with a dying battery, and a half bottle of water.

"According to his cell phone pings, he's at about the two-thousand-foot level," Chris added as the van's windshield wipers swiped at fat flakes of snow.

"Even though this is a hasty search, we're going to run containment," Jon said. "There's three trails in that area that could all be used to reach the spot where we think he's at. Since cell phone coordinates can be unreliable, we're going to break into three teams and go up all three routes. That way we won't end up chasing him if he gets confused or freaks out and starts hiking away from us."

"Didn't he get told to stay in one place?" Alexis asked.

"Of course," Jon said. "I told him myself. But people don't always do what they're told. Not when they're scared. Sometimes they decide they can't wait any longer and try to get themselves out. Once when I was sixteen, we got put out for a hasty search. This couple had called 9-1-1 and told us exactly where they were. But when we got there, there was a piece of paper with an arrow pointing down the trail." He smiled ruefully. "What was supposed to be a four-mile hike tuned into a twenty-five-mile slog in the middle of the night, with us basically chasing after them. We finally found them at a cabin they had broken into. Know what the first thing they said to us was?" He shook his head and snorted. " 'What took you so long?' "

Jon started working out logistics and naming people to teams. When Nick got assigned to Team One, he hid his grin. Led by Jon, Team One was going to take the most likely route, the one that matched up with the cell phone pings, the one George had started up before he got lost. When the van stopped to let them out, it was eight forty-five, and a light snow was falling.

They started out. Ahead of Nick, Jon was talking on his personal cell phone to George, trying to reassure him, telling him they would be there soon, telling him to stay put, telling him how to keep warm. Judging by Jon's end of the conversation, the guy was not dealing with things well. Jon finally had to end it to make sure they didn't run George's battery down to nothing.

In the light of Nick's headlamp, the snow was falling faster, the flakes getting smaller as the temperature dropped. Iraq was always hot, Nick was pretty sure about that, but still he could imagine he was with his unit, off on some sort of mission. Maybe they were an elite band of soldiers, hiking into the Alps to kill an evil master-mind in his mountain hideout, a man bent on destroying the world. All of them trained. All of them prepared to face death at any moment. Nick scanned the trees around them, pretending he might spot a sniper.

They hiked in silence, snowfall muffling their steps. Fifteen minutes passed, then a half hour. An hour. Two.

They smelled George before they saw him. Or smelled his desperate efforts to keep warm. A smoky odor that mingled cigarette smoke with scorched nylon.

They all lifted their heads, but Nick was the first to spot the wavering light. "I think that's him!" he called out, pointing. Without discussing it, they began to hurry, nearly running.

The fire was tiny, small enough that the big man who

was trying to keep warm was able to sit with his legs on either side.

When he saw them, he stood up and started to cry. He had a large round face and short dark hair. His cheeks were very red, and the rest of his face was nearly as white as the snow beginning to blanket the ground.

"George Hines?" Jon asked.

For an answer, he wrapped his arms around Jon, who made a startled "Oof!"

Despite Jon's advice, he had been sitting right on the ground, not even using branches or leaves to protect himself from the cold earth. The back of his pants were wet. They were jeans, and as SAR had drummed into Nick, cotton killed.

"Are you hurt at all?" Jon asked, untangling himself.

"I'm cold." George rubbed his hands up and down his arms. "I burned my backpack. I burned my smokes. And then I burned my hat."

His hat. Nick resisted the urge to roll his eyes. Why hadn't he just burned the rest of his clothes? How long would a hat burn, anyway? A minute? Two? And then you just had no hat and you weren't any warmer.

"These guys will set you up while I call in and let Base know you're okay," Jon said, as people began rooting through their packs. He unclipped the microphone from his jacket, pushed the button, and waited a second to speak. "Team One to Base." After a long pause, Jon tried again. "Team One to Base." Silence.

Max handed George an energy bar and got a hug in return that lifted him off his feet.

Meanwhile, Jon was unzipping layers. He pulled the

radio out of the rat pack. Radio reception could be affected by trees, the radio's position, the strength of the battery, water in the microphone, weather, rocky or hilly terrain—the list was endless. He had taught them that only when they had a straight line of sight less than five miles away were they guaranteed good radio reception.

Dimitri gave George two pairs of dry socks. George put his arms around Dimitri, who tried to worm out of it. "Not necessary for that, please, man." He still got a big hug.

Jon had climbed a nearby hill. Now he held the radio above his head with the antenna pointing straight up and repeated his call to Base. This time, he got a response.

"Go ahead, Team One."

"We've located the subject," Jon said as Jackie offered George a fleece pullover. Next to the big man, it looked comically small. Thinking he might have something larger, Nick started digging through his own pack. They all carried dry clothes, not just for themselves but also for any victims.

A crackle and then, "Copy. Can you give us a medical status and coordinates?"

Jon said, "Subject is mobile, cold and wet, in good spirits, and able to walk out."

In good spirits was an understatement. George was trading hugs for all kinds of things: a headlamp, a hand-held flashlight, a pair of gloves.

"Copy, Team One." A pause, and then, "Base to all teams, subject has been found. Please return to Base."

Teams Two and Three acknowledged the instructions.

Jon said, "Team One to Base."

"Go ahead."

"We have coordinates when you're ready."

"Go for coordinates."

Jon rattled off a string of numbers and the word *easting*.

"Copy. Go for northing."

Another string of numbers, followed by *northing*. It all meant nothing to Nick, since they hadn't covered coordinates yet.

"Copy. Go ahead and take care of your subject, and extract down when you're ready."

Jon grinned at his team. "Copy."

Nick gave George a large fleece. Even though he knew what was coming, he still was surprised by the fierceness of the other man's hug. He kept a poker face, but inside he was smiling.

"I feel like a kid on Christmas morning," George said as he pulled it on.

"And I've got a hat for you," Jon said as he rejoined them. "But don't go burning this one. I want it back in one piece."

It was six A.M. by the time they made it back down to the trailhead. It had taken them hours to return because a small landslide had blocked part of the trail and they had to slowly circumnavigate it. George Hines rested in the van for a bit and then drove himself back home to Beaverton while the SAR folks returned to the sheriff's office.

In the back seat of the van, sandwiched between Ruby and Alexis, Nick let himself grin like a fool. Sure, it could have been any of them who had spotted George. But it had been him.

It had been him.

He imagined his father's pride.

NO TIME TO BE SURPRISED

TIFFANY YEE WOKE IN THE MIDDLE OF THE night. It took her a minute to remember where she was. Someplace dark and warm and soft. Slowly, the realization seeped into her consciousness. She was in the guest room of that man's house, where she'd been a week or two earlier. It was the only place since she left home that she had been able to sleep, truly sleep. Two good nights out of sixty or so.

He was a nice enough guy, if a little weird. He hadn't put his hands on her. Yet. She was sure he would. Either that or talk about Jesus. Or maybe both. That was how it worked. A trade.

At least Tiffany existed for him. For many people she passed or who passed by her, she was like a ripple in the ocean. There and gone, without a trace.

Sleep grabbed her by the ankles and tried to pull her back down, but Tiffany wanted to know what time it was. How much longer she would be able to drift in the peaceful river of slumber. She reached under the pillow for her phone.

Only it was gone. More awake, she slid her hand back and forth, up and down, over the smooth, clean sheet. Nothing.

Tiffany sat up, electricity sparking in her veins. Her phone was her life. She would rather skip a meal or even a whole day of eating if it meant she could keep paying for her phone. Her brother called her on that phone. Maybe sometime he would say it was safe to come home.

Her caseworker called on that phone, too. And Tiffany put that number on job applications, although so far no one had called her, not since she had been caught getting high in the bathroom of the doughnut place while she was on break.

The inside of her head felt bruised and slushy, like someone had stuck a spoon in there and stirred. He had made her some Kahlua and cream earlier. She must have drunk more than she remembered. She made herself get out of bed. The world canted, and Tiffany had to brace herself against the bedpost until the dizziness passed. Then she ran her hands over the wall—as smooth and cool as the sheets—until she located the light switch. She flipped it up and stood blinking in the light.

Even the cheapest hotel rooms usually had bad framed prints on the wall. Here there was nothing. Just ivory-colored walls, tan-colored flat carpeting, and a big white bed, now smudged in places from her clothes. This guest room was more sterile than a hotel room. So sterile that she could smell herself.

She got down on her knees, ignoring how it made her head spin, and looked under the bed. Nothing. She pulled aside the small table that held only a lamp. Her phone was definitely gone. Still, she checked the pockets of her jeans and hoodie one more time.

Tiffany didn't know what time it was. Late. Maybe three in the morning. Finally she turned off the light and prepared to tiptoe down the hall. Had he taken it? But why would he want it? It was at least three generations behind, awkward and heavy compared with the phones rich people had. And he was rich. He threw away food without thinking about it, had big piles of new hardcover books, and kept the house as warm as if was spring outside, not closing in on winter.

Two days ago, three of her brother's friends had caught her digging in the big Dumpster outside Safeway, looking for food. It had been one of the lowest moments of the last few months, and there were many to choose from. But Tiffany could tell by the expression in their eyes that they thought this was absolutely the worst thing she had ever done. They didn't know she broke into cars, sometimes just to sleep, sometimes to steal iPods, laptops, or GPS units she could sell. They didn't know she couldn't shoplift from stores anymore—she stank so bad, everyone knew she was homeless. They didn't know she was on heroin and any Xanax or Valium she could steal. They didn't know that she had once found a gun in a shopping cart under the freeway and thought about killing herself, before hiding it in some bushes and making herself walk away.

Her brother's friends were good boys, though. One of them pressed three limp dollar bills into her hand and told her to buy herself something to eat at Mickey D's. She hadn't even had to ask for money, although she was getting pretty good at it by now. The combination of her baby

149

face and a sign that read TRYING TO GET HOME usually worked, bringing her pity and a few bucks.

Sometimes people just gave her food, like they were doing her a favor, but what she really needed was money. For drugs, sure, but for other stuff, too. Could she trade a hamburger for tampons? Or credit on her cell phone? TriMet bus fare? You couldn't buy toothpaste or socks or a comb with a hamburger. All you could do was eat it. You couldn't even save it for later.

Tiffany crept down the hall. Had she left her phone in the bathroom?

When she got to the end, her eyes caught a faint glow downstairs.

It was the man. He had told her to call him Mr. Smith. He was sitting at the dining room table. In front of him was her phone. He was bent over it, occasionally tapping his index finger.

Her phone was personal. More personal than Tiffany's body, which hardly felt like it belonged to her anymore. But her texts, her emails, her photos, her contacts, her notes—those were hers, and hers alone.

"What are you doing with my phone?" She had meant to say it in a voice that would echo through the whole house, but instead it came out little more than a whisper. "Give it back."

He barely turned to glance up at her, then went back to looking at her phone. She made it down the stairs—holding tight to the handrail for balance—and went up to him with her hand outstretched.

With a swipe of his finger, he made whatever he had been looking at disappear.

"What was that? What's on my phone that I don't know about?"

"Nothing that hurt you." His expression was pleasant. Benign. "Just a little tracker, that's all."

It took Tiffany a moment to figure out what he meant. Why were her thoughts so muddy? So muddled?

"Wait . . . you've been tracking me?"

"I'm interested in homeless girls. Where they go during the day, where they congregate, where they sleep."

"I'm not 'girls.' I'm me."

"Yes, but you're still part of a larger class."

"You could just ask, you know?" Tiffany tried to look haughty, but her face didn't feel like it was entirely within her control.

He tilted his head, regarding her calmly. "But would you tell me the truth? Always?"

"No. Because it's none of your business." Tiffany refused to let another person own her. She chose what she let other people see, other people know, other people touch.

"Right. Which is why I slipped a little piece of software into your phone. So I could see where you go, where you sleep. Your habits, diurnal and nocturnal. And don't worry, it's gone. I just deleted it."

"Okay," Tiffany said, not sure if it was. Not sure what to say. She held out her hand again.

He stood up and gave her the phone with one hand. With the other, he slipped a cord around her neck and stepped behind her.

Tiffany didn't even have time to be surprised.

HIS NEXT VICTIM

RUBY'S PARENTS HAD THOUGHT SHE WAS spending the night with Alexis. It was even sort of true.

"I'm glad you guys can still be friends," her mom had said.

Ruby hadn't met her eyes, but then again, Ruby hardly looked anyone straight in the eye. She was playing the role of Good Daughter, obedient, dutiful, grateful.

Now it was 6:47 A.M., and after hiking all night, nearly everyone in the SAR van was asleep. Even Jon was out, slumped against the front passenger side window. From the back seat where she was between Alexis and Nick, Ruby was keeping an eye on Chris's driving. He seemed to still have appropriate reflexes. But at sixty-five miles an hour, things could go south very fast. To soothe herself, she ran her finger up and down the seam of her Gore-Tex hiking pants.

She had thought Alexis was asleep too, but then the other girl spoke in a whisper. "I saw that they arrested that guy. The one we identified."

"And they had our pictures in the paper," Nick whispered from the other side of Ruby.

Their three heads were now so close together that Ruby could smell their breaths. She was chewing Japanese sour-melon-flavored gum, so she hoped hers smelled better than theirs did.

"What if it wasn't him?" she asked.

"Who else would it be?" Alexis screwed up her face. "We know he was there, and we know he had a reason to kill her."

"And remember how nervous he seemed?" Nick added.

"I'm not saying he wasn't growing pot," Ruby whispered. "That could explain the nervousness. But killing a girl, that's a very different kind of crime."

She had tried to picture it. Miranda hiking up the trail, somehow finding the marijuana plants. Maybe she had heard Adams talking to someone and followed the sound of his voice. And then at some point, something had gone terribly wrong, and he had slipped the cord of that duffel bag around her neck, pulling it tighter and tighter while she dug her fingers into her own flesh, trying to escape.

"I did find out something weird about Miranda today." Alexis looked at the time on her phone and let out a little bark of a laugh. "I guess I mean yesterday."

"What?" Ruby's heartbeat quickened.

"I heard that she was an oogle."

"What's an oogle?" Nick whispered.

"Kids who like to pretend they're homeless."

"*Homeless?*" Ruby forgot to keep her voice down. Alexis frowned, but no one else in the van stirred. Only

Chris glanced in the rearview mirror and then back at the freeway.

"Then that makes two." She straightened up. "Just like the girl in Washington Park I told you about. Detective Harriman said she didn't have anything in common with Miranda Wyatt. But if you're right, that means there are two dead homeless girls."

"But she only *pretended* she was homeless," Alexis said.

Ruby's mind was whirling with possibilities. In her gut, she knew this was more than a coincidence. "A killer might not be able to tell the difference between a real homeless girl and one who's pretending."

"Wait a second. Can we go back to the beginning?" Nick asked. "What was that word you said again? And why would anyone want to pretend to be homeless?"

"I guess real homeless people call kids who pretend they're homeless 'oogles.'" Alexis shrugged. "As for why, I don't really get it. Maybe she was bored. Maybe she thought it was cool. Or maybe she was just trying to make some money panhandling. Have you guys seen her Facebook page?"

"I tried," Ruby said, remembering her frustration, "but I couldn't see more than that she had a Facebook account."

"Me too," Nick agreed.

"I could see more because a couple of kids who go to my school used to go to hers, so we have some mutual 'friends.'" Alexis made air quotes. "Alder Grove is basically a school for rich kids who aren't doing that well. They don't give grades, and it's pretty much impossible to get kicked out, because then they would lose your tuition payments. So Miranda might have been able to hang out downtown in the middle of the day, pretending to be homeless, and the school might not even have told her parents she wasn't in class."

"So what *was* on her Facebook page?" Ruby asked, her pulse quickening.

"My phone can't go on Facebook." Alexis held out her hand. "Give me your phone and I'll show you."

Ruby dug it out of her pocket and handed it over. Alexis typed and clicked and finally handed it back. Nick looked over Ruby's shoulder. He sucked in his breath when she clicked on a photo of the dead girl in black bra and panties, her hands raised in what might be a gang signal. The next picture showed Miranda standing in an abandoned house, garbage on the floor, tags on the wall, a brown bottle of some sort of liquor tilted to her lips. At least in this photo she had all her clothes on. Ruby scrolled through photo after photo, but like Nick, she couldn't understand why it would appeal to anyone. It all looked dirty and stupid and pointless.

"But why would she be in Forest Park?" Ruby focused on Miranda's slack face. She remembered the wind rustling through the leaves, the birds calling, the light slanting between the trunks. "A girl like Miranda Wyatt would never go to Forest Park on her own."

Nick shook his head. "She might not have been the kind of girl to go on hikes, but she so looks like the kind of girl who might be interested in scoring some free weed."

"And be willing to walk three or four miles to steal it?" Alexis countered. "When it's sold all over downtown and probably at her school?"

"And if she stole the pot, wouldn't the newspaper have said so?" Ruby asked, remembering the article. "All it said was that they thought she must have stumbled over the marijuana grow. But it has to have been pretty well hidden, since it sounds like it's been there a long time and no one else has found it."

"Maybe somebody showed her the way?" Nick said.

"But who would do that except that Jay Adams guy?" Ruby said. "And why would he show it to her and then strangle her? It doesn't make sense. And if he really killed her because she stumbled over it, it seems like he would have done it right at the grow. Why do it by the trail where her body was more likely to be found? And just think, there were no drag marks, no signs of a struggle. Nothing but that one footprint by her." Ruby bit her lip, resisting the urge to complain again.

"Maybe Adams carried her," Nick said. "He's a big guy, remember?"

Alexis had fallen silent, had not even seemed to be following their last few exchanges. Now she sat forward, her voice suddenly urgent. "So, Ruby, do you really think there's someone out there killing homeless girls? Someone else?"

"It's certainly indicative of a pattern." And serial killers were all about patterns.

"Because you know that guy we saw with the two dogs? The one who was running?"

Nick smiled at the mention of the dogs, but Ruby grew more alert. "Yes?"

"I saw him yesterday, downtown at the bus mall. And he was arguing with this one girl with black hair and tattoos on her face. I don't know for sure, but she looked homeless."

Ruby went absolutely still, remembering the leash in the runner's pocket. Remembering the red furrow around the dead girl's neck.

"Whoa," Nick said. "We should talk to Harriman."

Ruby shook her head. "I've tried talking to him. As far as he's concerned, he's got the right guy. And just because Alexis saw the runner arguing with some homeless girl downtown, that's not going to be enough to change his mind. We're going to have to bring him proof."

"And how exactly are we going to do that?" Nick asked.

The answer had already popped into Ruby's head. "My dad's a runner. He runs the same route at the same time every night. From what I've seen, a lot of runners are that way. And those two dogs must need to be exercised every day. If we went back to the same spot at the same time on the same day of the week as when we first met him, I think there's a good chance we would see him again."

Nick nodded. "And then we could ask him a few questions."

"And how's that going to work?" Alexis said in a tone even Ruby could tell was sarcastic. "You're going to say, 'Are you the serial killer?' and he's going to say, 'Why, yes, I am!' I don't think so."

Ruby felt like she had when she realized Alexis was trying to keep her distance. If she liked somebody, she knew she tended to latch on like a crab and not let go. But when they both first joined SAR, Alexis had made Ruby feel not so lonely. They had sat together at every class, slept side by side every training weekend. Ruby was convinced she had found someone who would be her friend forever. Someone who could help her mix with normal people. Alexis had encouraged Ruby to tell stories, had merged her gracefully into other people's conversations. Around Alexis, Ruby was no longer the weird girl hiding in the back of the room. Instead, Ruby had begun to turn into the part she was playing: Best Friend.

But then Alexis had begun to pull away, and Ruby had no idea why.

"We could follow him," Ruby managed to say evenly. "Get his license plate number or his address. Once we know that, we can go online. There's websites you can go to that will give you all kinds of information for twenty-five or thirty bucks. Once we have a name and an address and maybe some criminal history on him, then I think Detective Harriman will listen to us."

"I don't know. . . ." Alexis's voice trailed off. But at least she didn't rule out the idea altogether.

"We should go there this afternoon and scope it out," Nick said. "Then we'll know where to hide on Tuesday."

"I can't," Alexis said. "There's something I have to do." She didn't elaborate. Ruby wondered if she was lying, then told herself that wasn't what was important here. Not anymore.

"Then Nick and I will go," Ruby said decisively. "We have to do something. Because if the cops are wrong, then right now this guy is out looking for his next victim."

ONLY AIR

THE PHONE WOKE ALEXIS. SHE SNATCHED it up from where she had plugged it in next to her bed.

"Mom?" She had said the same thing yesterday afternoon, only it had turned out to be Mitchell telling her about the call-out.

"Alexis?" a guy said. Not Mitchell.

And then it clicked. Bran. Alexis put her free hand on her chest and willed her heart to slow. "Yeah, it's me."

"Did I wake you up?"

"Don't worry. I had to get up anyway because the phone was ringing."

Bran groaned. "Pretty lame joke. You sound like my grandfather."

"It's the best I can do after getting"—Alexis looked at the clock—"four hours of sleep. SAR pulled a lost hiker out of the Gorge last night, and we didn't get back until this morning."

Alexis hadn't given much thought to what it would

actually be like. How it would feel to locate someone who was lost. To save somebody.

But this morning a crying George Hines had hugged her in the parking lot, even though she hadn't even been on the team that found him. As he wetly mumbled thanks into her ear, it had hit her that SAR really saved lives. It wasn't like it had been on the training weekends, endless tramping around, pretending to find someone who was lost. Walking and walking and walking, trudging past one tree that pretty much looked the same as the next. No, this had been the real thing. If Search and Rescue hadn't been there, it was possible George Hines would have died.

Finding Miranda's body had been awful. Looking for evidence that would lead to her killer had been both tedious and a terrible reminder of the reality of her death.

But last night Alexis and the others had been a team, trained and ready to save. When she had felt the wet press of George's cheek against her own, she had realized it was all worth it: the boredom and the cold and all the math you had to use to figure out exactly where you were. They had saved a man's life.

Now Bran said, "Really? Way to go! I love trauma intervention, and what we do is really important, but we're always just going to be picking up the pieces." He took a breath. "Anyway, I wanted to check in and see how you were doing. To see if you were sleeping any better than you were the other night. Only it turns out that by calling you, I've actually caused the problem I was worried about."

"It *is* a bit ironic," Alexis agreed teasingly. She sat up, even though every bit of her longed to stretch out again, pull the covers over her head to block out the daylight, and fall back asleep.

He echoed her thoughts. "I should let you get back to sleep."

"No. I need to get up." As she spoke, Alexis heaved herself to her feet. "There's things I've got to do today." Not her homework, although some buried part of her knew she really did need to tackle it. But the most important thing was finding her mom.

"Then can I buy you a cup of coffee to help you wake up? And to make up for the sleep I made you miss?"

She never should have texted him. It was better to keep people at arm's length. Alexis opened her mouth to say no.

"That would be great."

When she walked into Perk Up, Bran was already there. Mara leaned over the counter and said in a low voice, "Have you found your mom yet, honey?"

Alexis froze. Had Bran heard? But he had his back to them, seemingly engrossed by the pastry case.

"No. Not yet." She gave Mara a strained smile and hoped that the other woman got that she didn't want to talk about it.

Mara made them both sixteen-ounce lattes in tall clear glasses. Alexis's was topped with a heart made of foam, Bran's with a leaf. And after some discussion with both Alexis and Mara, Bran also got a cranberry-walnut scone and a croissant filled with chocolate. As soon as they sat down, he split both of them and slid her halves over on a napkin. Alexis noticed he gave her the largest of each.

She took a deep breath. "So did you call me because of TIP? Is this something you're supposed to do?"

He looked down at his coffee. "It's not exactly in the manual, no." His eyes flicked back up to her. "So why did that lady ask about your mom?"

It was like nearing the bottom of a dark staircase and not knowing if there was one more step. If Alexis put her foot out, would she meet firm ground or only air?

"If I tell you something, do you have to report it to anyone?"

Bran held her gaze with his stormy gray eyes. "If it's about hurting yourself or someone else, then yes. Other than that, no."

"It's not anything like that," Alexis said. For a distracted moment, she wondered just how bad TIP got. "It's my mom. I don't know where she is."

"What do you mean? Do you think something happened to her?"

"I don't know. But I'm worried it might have."

"Do you think someone hurt her?" His brows drew together. "Or that she's been in an accident?"

"I don't know enough to know." Her sigh was so deep and long it felt like it came from the soles of her feet. "I guess anything's possible."

"Where's the last place you know she was for sure?"

"Our apartment. We were arguing Wednesday night, and she ran out." In her memory, she heard the sound of the slamming door. "Only she never came back."

"Have you called her cell phone?"

"She left it behind." Alexis remembered the horror she had felt when she called it and heard it ringing underneath the coffee table.

"How about her friends or people she works with? Have they heard from her?"

Alexis hesitated and then said in a rush, "To be honest, she doesn't have those, either. She hasn't worked in a long time."

"Do you have any guess as to where she might be?"

"I don't know. Downtown, maybe? See, my mom is, um, sort of"—she forced herself to say it—"mentally ill." It felt painful but good, like throwing up after suffering for hours from a queasy stomach. "She's on meds, but they don't work that well, and she doesn't like the way they make her feel. So sometimes she stops taking them."

His expression didn't change. "What kind of mentally ill?"

"I've never really been told, but I think she's bipolar. All I know is that when she's off her meds, she's either nonstop or she's not moving. Like she would always read to me at night when I was little. That's normal, right? You read until the kid gets sleepy and then you're done. Only that's not how it worked with my mom when she wasn't taking her meds. I'd be closing my eyes, and she'd be poking me and telling me I had to look at the pictures, asking me to sound out the words. She'd be pouting because I kept falling asleep. And there can be days when she doesn't seem to sleep at all."

"That sounds scary." Bran lightly touched her wrist, then set his hand next to hers on the table.

Alexis nodded. "But my mom can also be so fun. I

remember when I was little, sometimes she would spend all day with me making sugar cookies and icing them. She didn't care if we made a mess or if we ate cookies for breakfast, lunch, and dinner. And she used to take me to the store and let me buy as many stickers and as much Play-Doh as I wanted." Raising her glass, she rested her cheek against the warmth.

"That part doesn't sound so bad."

"Right before she took off, she was convinced the people on TV were talking about her. And she thought I was one of them or something." Alexis's voice broke. "That's why she left."

But her mom didn't have anyplace to go except the streets. What if Ruby was right and a serial killer was targeting homeless women? Because right now, that might be just what her mother was.

"Are you afraid of what might have happened to her?" Bran asked.

Alexis nodded. And then she burst into tears.

THE CRUEL CURVE

RUBY WATCHED NICK TURN IN A CIRCLE IN the small clearing in Forest Park. "It was right here that we saw the runner," he insisted, pointing at an open spot between the trees. "I'm sure of it." The park was a patchwork of western hemlock, western red cedar, grand fir, Douglas fir, maples, and alders. The biggest firs were fire-scarred, perhaps a couple of hundred years old.

Ruby didn't put much energy into arguing with Nick. She knew he was wrong. "No it wasn't. Where we met him was farther back. There were two Doug firs grow-ing right next to each other, with an alder in front of them." She had also noted the time they had met the run-ner: 5:16 P.M. While she didn't expect that they would see him at three thirty on a Sunday afternoon, right now they were laying the groundwork so that, with a little luck, they could spot him Tuesday, exactly one week after Miranda had been murdered.

Their plan was to come here the day after tomorrow after school, hide themselves away in the brush, and wait for him to appear. Once he did, the chase would be on.

When he left the park, they might be able to follow the runner in Ruby's car or, if they were lucky and he lived nearby, straight to his house.

They walked farther up the trail. The mud sucked at the soles of their boots, but Ruby's ears were tuned to the trills and calls of the birds. She picked out the song of a black-headed grosbeak. From the top of a hemlock, a chickadee let out a three-note song.

They were almost on top of the older man before they saw him. Ruby put her hand out to stop Nick from blundering forward. He was standing absolutely still, an expensive-looking camera pointing at the top of the tallest tree. As Ruby watched, the camera lens silently lengthened. She followed the angle with her eyes until she spotted his target: a magnificent Cooper's hawk with slate-gray wings and a pale breast and belly. The shutter clicked rapidly, then the bird lifted its wings and flapped off. The man let the camera thump against his chest, next to a pair of binoculars.

He caught sight of them and smiled. "We meet again," he said. "Hopefully under happier circumstances."

"I remember you," Ruby said. "We talked about bird-watching."

"That's right. I'm Caleb Becker." They all shook hands.

"I'm Ruby McClure, and this is Nick Walker. We were both part of the search and rescue group looking for that missing man."

Becker pressed his lips together and shook his head. "The police told me your group found someone, but it wasn't the person you were looking for. Some poor dead girl."

"We're actually the ones who found her," Nick said.

"I'm so sorry." He shook his head. "That must have been awful."

Ruby barely heard him. All her attention was on his camera. "You had that camera with you that day, didn't you?"

His forehead wrinkled. "Why, yes, as a matter of fact, I did."

Excitement bubbled in her chest. "Did you take pictures that showed any of the people who were here?" Detective Harriman had said the police hadn't been able to locate the runner with the dogs or the homeless man from that day on the trail. Photos of them might make a difference.

"Sorry. The police already asked me that, but I'm afraid the answer was no. I don't take snapshots. I'm only interested in these beautiful creatures." He waved one hand at the treetops.

"Oh." Ruby's excitement deflated as quickly as it had expanded.

He cocked his head. "Besides, I read that the police have already arrested someone for the murder."

"We talked to him," Nick said. "I was as close to him as I am to you. He was super nervous. Now we know why."

"I'm glad I didn't run into him. The only things I want to see in these woods are the birds." He smiled at Ruby. "You've probably noticed how alive the woods are today."

"I've spotted a raven and a chickadee," she said. "What have you seen?"

"It's been a good day." He ticked the answers off on his fingers. "Chickadees, woodpeckers, scrub jay, Steller's jay, the dark-eyed junco, the spotted towhee, and one of my favorites, the golden-crowned kinglet."

"Golden-crowned kinglet?" Nick repeated with a laugh.

"Fat little fellows with a yellow streak on the tops of their heads." Becker ran his fingers along the top of his own thick white hair. "Beautiful plumage. Very striking."

"I found this feather," Nick said, holding out a long narrow black and white feather with an orange-red shaft. Ruby hadn't noticed him pick it up. "Do you know what it is?"

"Northern flicker," Becker said immediately. "Red-shafted. There's also a yellow-shafted variety, but they're less common."

Ruby let out a little huff. She could have told Nick what it was, but he hadn't even thought to ask her.

"You can't keep it, Nick," she said. She knew some people collected bird feathers the way her mom collected owl figurines. "Under the Migratory Bird Treaty Act of 1918, possession of bird feathers is a federal crime."

Nick snorted in disbelief. "Are you serious? It's not like I killed a bird and pulled out its feathers. I *found* it."

"Ruby's right," Becker said. "Nearly every bird is protected. It's left over from when whole species went extinct so ladies could wear huge hats decorated with feathers. Personally, I think it's a tad outdated. Although it's not like they actually have the cops out hunting people who like to collect pretty feathers. They've got better things to do. As you two well know." He frowned and then turned to Ruby, his expression lightening. "Since you're a fellow birder, have you heard the news? The swifts have finally been sighted up north. They should start showing up here in the next two or three days."

Ruby felt a huge grin spread across her face. On their migration down to their winter home in Central America, swifts flew nonstop all day, even eating on the fly. They alighted at night only to rest. Every fall for the past twenty years, thousands of swifts had stopped to roost in the old brick chimney on Portland's Chapman Elementary School. But so far this year there had been less than a handful. Everyone worried it was yet another sign of global warming.

"I can't wait to see them." She clapped her hands. "It doesn't feel like it's really fall without the swifts." Recalling their previous conversation, she asked, "So have you seen your northern spotted owl yet?"

"Not yet, but I still keep looking. Good things are worth the wait." He took the digital camera from around his neck. "Like that Cooper's hawk I was taking pictures of a minute ago."

He pressed a button and handed them the camera. The photo was in perfect focus. Above the cruel curve of its black beak, the bird's red eyes stared down alertly.

"It looks like an eagle," Nick said.

Becker clapped him on the shoulder. "Very perceptive. It's a raptor. So are eagles. The very top of the food chain." A smile curved his lips. "I'm saying 'it,' but this is more than likely a female. Female raptors are usually much bigger than the males."

"Seriously?" Nick said.

"If it's any consolation, male birds of all types usually have the better plumage. Not like humans, where the most interesting-looking specimens are invariably female."

"She's a beauty." Ruby was filled with a quiet, buzzing joy. It was such a pleasure to meet an adult happy to discuss one of her pet subjects. Kids her own age didn't care about birds.

She handed back the camera, but as he took it, the older man lost his balance on the uneven ground. He had to steady himself on Ruby's shoulder, and then he grabbed her backpack for balance. By the time he was stable again, he was red-faced and embarrassed. Not meeting her eyes, he straightened Ruby's backpack, even adjusting a zipper, and then patted her shoulder. "Oh my, I'm so sorry about that."

"That's okay," Ruby said hurriedly. It must be terrible to get old and weak.

But then again, it would be even more terrible to die long before you ever had a chance to get old.

CHAPTER 32

SUNDAY

OUTSIDER

EVEN WORSE THAN CRYING WAS HAVING someone see you cry. In a desperate effort to stop her tears, Alexis bit her lower lip, widened her eyes, and blinked rapidly. Bran leaned forward and took both her hands in his. Pulling free, she put them over her face. Under her palms, her cheeks were hot. If only she could just disappear.

A chair scraped back and then a strong arm encircled her shoulders as Bran crouched next to her.

"Hey, it'll be okay," he said in a low voice next to her ear.

"You don't know that," she said from behind the shelter of her hands. "Nobody knows that."

His sigh stirred the hairs on the back of her neck. "That's true," he agreed, surprising her. "But I do know that it's possible to live through things that you honestly thought would kill you. You can even come out stronger on the other side."

Right now, Alexis felt anything but strong. "How do you know that?"

After a pause, Bran said softly, "Someday I'll tell you." He squeezed her shoulder. "But not today. Today is about helping you find your mom."

What was she doing? Alexis didn't even really know this guy, and here she was falling apart in front of him. And if she did let him help her? Either they wouldn't find her mom and Bran would worry about her being on her own, or they would and he would see for himself just how crazy she was. What if he decided it was his duty as a member of TIP to report her home situation to children's services?

Alexis took her hands away, grabbed her napkin, swiped it across her eyes, then pushed herself to her feet. Bran's arm fell loosely to her waist as he stood up, too. She stepped away and turned to face him. "This is something I really need to do by myself. For one thing, my mom doesn't like strangers." Which was only partly true. There were times her mom craved an audience. But she was also wary of anyone who wanted to fix her.

"I just want to help you." Bran's eyes locked onto hers.

She looked away. She ignored Mara, who had stopped loading cups into the dishwasher and was giving her a look that basically said, "Are you crazy?"

"You can help," Alexis said, "by letting me do this on my own."

Back at home, Alexis paced the small living room, trying to figure out how she could find her mom. She had already tried looking downtown and gotten nowhere. But she had been an outsider dressed in nice clothes that no one could tell had come from a thrift store. Maybe if homeless people thought she was one of them, they would open up more.

In her mom's closet she found a shapeless brown sweater with stretched-out sleeves and a pair of faded green cargo pants. Once she changed, Alexis checked herself in the mirror. What with the bags under her eyes, her lack of makeup, and her crazy hair from running around in the wind and drizzle, she already looked the part of a homeless girl. Bran must have thought she was pathetic. No wonder he had been so nice. It had probably all been driven by pity.

The photo of her mom was still in her backpack. Alexis added two granola bars in case she got hungry. She tucked her cell phone into her pocket, but after putting a couple of dollars into her other pocket, she left her wallet on the counter. No ID meant nothing to contradict any story she told. On a scrap of paper, she wrote, "Mom—gone to find you. If you come home, call me!" Not trusting her mom's memory, Alexis scribbled her phone number on the bottom.

She decided to walk. Even in their own neighborhood, there were plenty of homeless people who might have seen her mom: smoking on curbs, reading Bibles under tarps, and lugging black plastic garbage bags full of belongings. Alexis was a child of the city, used to ignoring them, used to crossing the street, used to not making eye contact.

But now her eyes had been opened.

The first person Alexis approached was a plump black woman pushing a shopping cart loaded with plastic-wrapped bundles. Despite the cold, the woman wore flip-flops, a short-sleeved shirt, and cropped pants that dug into her full calves.

"Excuse me." Alexis pulled out her mom's photo. "Have you seen this woman?"

The woman looked from it to Alexis and back again. "That must be your mama. You look so much alike."

Her throat swelled closed. All she could do was nod.

"No, I haven't seen her, honey. Sorry."

Alexis moved on, stopping every now and then to ask people who didn't scare her too much. More homeless were scattered under the on-ramp to the bridge. But if any of them had seen Alexis's mom, they weren't saying.

At the far end of the bridge, a girl sat cross-legged on the sidewalk, her back against a metal fence. She wore a navy blue American Apparel hoodie, jeans, and scuffed boots. Next to her were a blue backpack and a bottle of Coke Zero. In front of her feet a sign simply said PLEASE HELP.

"Hey." Alexis held out her mom's photo, which was already crumpled. "I'm looking for this lady. Have you seen her?"

The girl took it without speaking. While she looked at the photo, Alexis looked down at the top of her head. Her black hair was scraped back into a cross between a ponytail and a bun.

"Yeah, I have seen her around," she said, rolling her Rs.

"Wait—what—you have?" Alexis felt a jolt of electricity.

"Not today."

"Then when?"

The girl shrugged. "Maybe yesterday? Or the day

before." And just as Alexis was beginning to doubt, she added, "She was talking about God. And I think she was barefoot."

"That's her. That's my mom." Instead of feeling relieved, Alexis felt like she had just been punched in the stomach. She doubled over.

The girl leaned forward and patted the back of Alexis's head. "It's okay," she murmured. "It's okay."

Alexis straightened, blinking back tears. "It's just that's the first I've heard of her in a few days."

The girl's face clouded. "Did you guys get separated by the shelter?"

Alexis nodded. It didn't feel as much like a lie if she didn't say it out loud.

"That's such bull!" the other girl exploded. "I hate it when they do that! Like once you're over thirteen, it's okay to separate you. But if you don't have your family, you don't have nothing." She held out her hand. It was callused, the nails broken to different lengths. "My name's Raina."

She took her hand. "Alexis. My mom's name is Tanya. I can't find her, and I don't know where to look. I'm really worried about her."

Raina gazed at her more closely. "You haven't been out here very long."

"Um, we haven't."

"Then you might not know all the places to check." The other girl got to her feet. "So let's go see if we can find her."

Alexis hesitated. She hadn't been looking for a helper. But then she nodded.

"Which shelter were you staying at?" Raina asked.

She hadn't thought this story through. "A private one run by a church. On the East Side."

"And they said they didn't have any more room for adults, right? Like your mom isn't just as vulnerable as you." Raina shot her a look. "Maybe more."

"She has some issues," Alexis said. Which she wished was a lie.

"Everything's closed right now." Raina leaned down to pick up her things. "And people aren't allowed to wait outside the doors until they open, because it bugs the other businesses. But there are other places where she might be."

With Raina as her guide, Alexis went on a tour of the various areas where homeless people congregated. The library, McDonald's ("They're pretty chill about letting you charge your phone"), a church basement. Over and over, Alexis asked people about her mom, showed her picture. A few thought they might have seen her, but no one was as specific as Raina.

The red brick steps of Pioneer Courthouse Square were empty except for homeless people. The day was too cold for anyone who had anyplace else to go to be outside.

"When I first came to Portland, I refused to sit," Raina said after they finished talking to a man who had just a few teeth left in his mouth, even though he looked like he was only in his mid-thirties. "It was too embarrassing. I would have rather been dead on my feet than sit on the sidewalk and have people guess I was homeless. But you know what?" She shrugged. "There's no hiding it. Somehow people always just know."

Alexis had a pretty good idea how. Raina didn't really look that dirty, but she smelled funky.

"What time is it?" Raina asked.

Alexis checked her phone and told her.

"Day services is open. Let's go check it out."

Once they got there, Alexis followed Raina in. It was a big open room with lockers in the back. On one side was a line of people waiting to use the three computers. On the other side of the room, people were watching a movie on TV. In the middle was a pool table, its green felt matted and scarred from years of play. Everywhere people were curled up on couches or just the floor, trying to nap despite the noise.

Raina wasn't shy about asking people if they had seen Alexis's mom, even those who looked sound asleep. Each time, Alexis handed over the photo. But no one recognized her, not even the staff workers, who presumably weren't groggy from lack of sleep or previous ingestion of illicit substances.

Finally Alexis leaned against the wall. Next to her a framed piece of paper read NO DRUGS, NO SEX, NO VIOLENCE. In the corner, three photographs were tacked on the wall. She moved closer.

"Who are these people?" she asked Raina.

"That's the memorial wall." She pointed at the first picture, which showed a black kid with high cheekbones. The photo had been enlarged over and over, so the face was composed of a series of dots like a piece of modern art. "He was hit by a car." Raina's finger moved to the next photo, a blond man with a blank face. "He was found dead in an alley, but I never did hear from what." The third was a girl with crooked yellow bangs and crooked yellow teeth. "She died right on that couch over there. Heroin overdose. One of the staff tried to wake her up, and she was gone." All the photos had messages scrawled on the edges. The girl had the most.

It was bad enough that there was someone out there, killing girls like this one. It was worse that they were killing themselves.

"I'm thinking there's one more place we could look," Raina said. "Hell."

"What?" Alexis took a step back.

"It's an underground parking lot. We call it Hell. It's a good place to sleep, since so many people forget about it. If you go to the bottom level, there's hardly ever anyone parked there."

"Then let's go to Hell," Alexis said.

The parking lot on Fourth Avenue didn't have an attendant, just a machine that took credit cards. They ducked under the yellow arm and then Alexis followed Raina, spiraling down, down, down. The bottom level held only a single car.

Someone lay curled up on a bed of cardboard next to a Dumpster, with a coat pulled over the head. Alexis knew that coat! She had bought it for herself at Goodwill last year, but her mom had worn it more. Already relieved, Alexis bent down, lifted the edge, and raised it up.

But the woman who started up on one elbow, cursing, was not her mom.

THE DEATH OF TIFFANY YEE

AS SOON AS THE ALARM ON HER TABLET went off, Ruby rolled over and grabbed it. The tablet was one of three computers she owned. Four, if you counted her phone.

Propping herself up on her pillow, she didn't look at her texts or emails or Facebook, at least not at first. Ruby always checked the latest crime stories, starting in Portland, and then in the United States.

Her first stop was KATU.com. Since it was a Monday morning, there were lots of crime-related headlines. Even criminals must have more free time to get into trouble on weekends.

**WOMAN'S BODY FOUND IN COLUMBIA RIVER
CAR THEFT SUSPECT TRACKED DOWN, BIT BY K9
SUSPECTS SOUGHT IN WALMART THEFT RING
PORTLAND GYM OWNER TURNS TABLES ON ATTACKER**

When Ruby clicked on the link for the body discovered in the river, it turned out that it had been found wearing a lifejacket, and an empty kayak was floating nearby. Probably an accidental death. And what interested Ruby were murders.

She returned to the main page. Only then did she notice a smaller headline toward the bottom:

RUNAWAY'S BODY FOUND IN MACLEAY PARK

Ruby's heart started to race. She knew that park. It was actually on the outer edge of Forest Park, a finger of green that started near downtown and then pointed into the West Hills. She clicked on the link.

Authorities are seeking the public's help in an investigation into the death of Tiffany Yee, a 16-year-old runaway whose body was discovered early Sunday morning in Macleay Park. Police call the girl's death suspicious. Officers were dispatched about 8 a.m. to the park on the report of a dead body, said Sgt. Gene Paulson, spokesperson for the Portland Police Bureau.

Based on what the arriving officers saw, homicide detectives and criminal investigators were called to the scene, he said. Nearby residents said the park is generally quiet.

The Roosevelt High School honors student reportedly ran away from home in early September. The school district will have mental health personnel on-site today for all students and staff.

Detectives asked anyone who has information about Yee's death or her whereabouts over the last eight weeks, or who has witnessed suspicious activity in the area, to contact the homicide department.

There was no word on any possible suspects in the case.

Tiffany Yee.

With a sick certainty, Ruby knew that this girl was another victim of the same person who had killed Miranda and the girl found in Washington Park. The question was *when* had she been killed? If the autopsy said she had died before Friday evening, then Detective Harriman might still argue that Jay Adams had killed her, even though Macleay Park was nowhere near the marijuana patch Adams had supposedly killed Miranda Wyatt to protect. But if Tiffany Yee had died after that, Detective Harriman might consider that the same person could be responsible for all three deaths—and that maybe Adams hadn't killed Miranda after all.

As if in rebuttal, Ruby heard Detective Harriman's voice in her head. "Serial killers have types. They don't just go around killing anyone."

The frustrating thing was that he was right. One of the most basic tenets of how serial killers operated was that they almost always targeted victims of the same race as themselves. She thought of Ted Bundy, the guy who had killed dozens of girls in the 1970s. Nearly all of them had been white college students with long dark hair parted in the middle.

But now there were three dead girls found in Portland parks. A black girl, possibly homeless, and still unidentified. A rich white girl who liked to pretend she was homeless. And now a runaway with a Chinese last name who was from a high school in one of Portland's poorest neighborhoods.

As Ruby got into the shower, she ran through possibilities. If there was just one killer, he had to have a reason for what he was doing. It had to make sense to him, even if it didn't to anyone looking on from the outside. And that reason had drawn him to three very different girls.

Alexis had seen the runner arguing with a girl who looked homeless. Maybe he was tired of the street kids who sometimes partied in Forest Park, who lit illegal bonfires and went off the paths, destroying delicate vegetation.

Still, Ruby felt like she was missing something. Something beyond being homeless that might tie the three girls together.

What if it wasn't the runner at all? Maybe it was someone who worked with the homeless or volunteered with them. Someone in a position like that would certainly have easy access to victims. Or what if it was someone who was homeless, like the guy with the dreads? What reason had he had for being up there? Maybe he had talked Miranda into walking up that path and then come back down—alone.

It could even be someone pretending to be a cop. The Hillside Stranglers had posed as undercover police officers and "arrested" prostitutes. In addition to tricking college girls by pretending to have a broken arm, Ted Bundy had also posed as a cop. And a serial killer in Florida had actually *been* a cop.

Ruby was lost in thought when she came down to

breakfast. Her parents were sitting on the couch. Together. Not sitting at the dining room table. Not eating breakfast. Not reading the paper.

But her mom did have a section of the paper in her lap.

"What's wrong?" Ruby asked. Her parents liked their routines nearly as much as she did.

Her mom held it up. "Ruby. Why did you lie to us?"

She realized it was the issue of the paper that had SAR's photo in it. "What are you talking about?" The strangled tone of her voice gave her away.

"What's wrong is that you lied to us," her mom said.

Her dad shook his head. "We told you you had to quit SAR. Instead you went out and did the very thing that we most didn't want you to do."

"Pam at the office told me she saw your photo in the paper, the paper you said you couldn't find in the driveway." Her mom shook it. "Which I found in your room while you were in the shower."

Ruby stuffed her fists in her pockets so she wouldn't pick up one of her mom's stupid owl figurines from the bookcase and smash it. "You were going through my room?" When she was getting dressed, she had noticed that her wastebasket had been moved, but she'd been too preoccupied to think about what it meant.

"You are our child." Her mom raised her chin. "Your safety is our responsibility."

"I am not a child. I'm sixteen." In some countries, she could be married by now. Even have a child or two of her own.

Her dad held out his hand. "Give me your keys."

"What?"

He enunciated every word. "You're grounded. Give me your keys and your cell phone. You will go to school on the bus, and you will come directly back home on the bus, and that's all you will do. And I will call SAR and tell them you have to pull out."

She stepped back, her hand going protectively to her pocket. "What? Why?"

"We trusted you, Ruby." Her dad shook his head. "We trusted you, and you lied to us."

"I'm sorry!" she yelled. "I'm sorry! Okay? I'm really sorry!" They couldn't take SAR away from her. Especially now. Didn't they know how important it was?

"Ruby." Her dad sighed. "You know that apologies don't count if you shout them."

"I only went because it's important. It might help the police catch a killer."

That was the wrong thing to say. She knew it as soon as she said it. "That's it," her mom said. "Your father is right. You're obsessed with death. And it's not healthy."

"What if I want to do this kind of stuff as a job?"

"You're sixteen years old," her dad said. "You're too young to know what you want. This is just an infatuation."

"We've signed you up for horseback riding lessons on Saturdays," her mom said, pasting on a smile even Ruby could tell was fake. "You always said you wanted to do that."

Ruby tried to think of a persona she could adopt with them, some role she could play that would make them relent. Instead she found herself stamping her foot like a child.

"It's not fair!" she yelled.

Her dad shook his head as he got up from the couch. "Life isn't fair, Ruby. You of all people should have figured that out by now."

THINGS CHANGE

WHEN ALEXIS WOKE UP, SHE DIDN'T KNOW where she was. She started to sit up but banged her head. Why was she so close to the ceiling? She realized she was on the top level of a bunk bed, one of two crammed into the small room. Only a few feet across from her, another girl was still asleep, one arm covering her eyes.

And then it all came back to her. Last night, she and Raina had spent the night at this shelter. They had stayed up until lights-out, hoping her mom would come in—or that Alexis would at least hear news of her. The closest she had come was one woman who thought she might have seen her mom a few days earlier.

It was like her mom had vanished.

Or maybe, a part of Alexis worried, someone had already turned her mom into another body in the woods. Just waiting to be found.

It had been hard enough to sleep with thoughts like that. And then when she had finally managed to drop off, the girl on the other bottom bunk had started tripping out, screaming that her wallet had been stolen by witches. The rest of them had huddled in their beds while the shelter workers tried to reason with the girl. They were finally reduced to just restraining her. Eventually an ambulance had been called and they had dragged the girl away, kicking and raging. Even once it was more or less quiet, Alexis hadn't been able to get back to sleep.

The door to their room opened. "Okay, girls, time to get up," a woman with a long gray braid said. In the bunk below hers, Alexis heard Raina groan.

Getting ready was a snap when you were already dressed. From one of the black plastic milk crates that doubled as cubbies, Alexis took her shoes and slipped them on, then picked up her coat and backpack. In her real life, she would be getting ready to go to school, but her real life was starting to feel as distant and surreal as one of the nightmares she'd had last night.

"Ready?" Raina asked with a yawn.

But in the main room, everyone was clustered in front of the memorial wall instead of the food. A new photo had joined the other three. A girl who looked Asian American, standing in this very same room.

Raina sucked in her breath. "Oh my God—Tiff? What happened to Tiff?"

"She's dead," another girl said bluntly. Her black hair was shaved down to bare scalp on one side. "Someone strangled her in a park."

"What?" A shock zipped down Alexis's spine. "When? What park?"

"Macleay. It's not far from here. I guess they found her yesterday morning."

Another dead homeless girl. Anxiety bubbled in Alexis's chest. A sour taste flooded the back of her tongue.

"People!" The woman with the braid clapped her hands. "I'm sorry, but we still have a schedule to keep. If you guys want breakfast, you need to eat now."

Slowly, people began to move to a table where pitchers of milk and juice and bins of cereal had been set out. There were two kinds—generic Cheerios and generic Wheaties— and when Alexis took a sip of her orange juice, it didn't taste quite right. She and Raina found a seat at a table.

"I can't believe Tiff is dead." Raina's mouth twisted. "I just saw her a few days ago."

"What was she like?" Was this what it was like for Bran, asking people about their losses?

"Sweet. Messed up."

"She's the third one."

"Third what?" Raina asked.

"Third homeless girl found strangled in a park." Alexis found Miranda's crumpled photo at the bottom of her backpack. "Did you know her? Because she was the second."

Raina put her hand to her chest. "Are you serious? I've seen her around downtown. Usually drunk or high. Sometimes begging for money and laughing about it afterward. But she wasn't really homeless, you know."

"Maybe the killer didn't know that."

Raina's eyes went wide.

"And there was a third girl, a black girl they found a few weeks ago in Washington Park. That's another reason I have to find my mom. Because someone is killing homeless girls. And you've seen my mom—she's only thirty-six, and she looks younger."

Around them, people started getting to their feet, picking up their things. The shelter was closing. While they were leaving, the workers told them to "Stay safe!" and cautioned them not to go anyplace with a stranger.

"You really think it was a stranger?" Raina asked Alexis once they were out on the sidewalk.

"What do you mean?"

"I'm thinking it might have been one of us. Who else knows homeless people better than another homeless person? And if we drop out of sight, nobody asks any questions."

Raina was walking slowly, and Alexis matched her pace. "Maybe," she said, thinking of the homeless guy they had met while they were searching for Bobby. But then she thought of the runner. "But maybe not. There's this one guy I've seen in Forest Park. That's where that Miranda girl's body was found. He was running there with his dogs on the day she was killed, and he was carrying the dogs' leashes in his pocket. And then a few days later, I saw him on the bus mall, arguing with another girl who looked homeless."

Raina took a half step back. "What does he look like?"

"Not like much of anything. Maybe five foot nine. Thin. Dark hair. Mid-thirties. He has these two dogs. Big ones. I've seen him once with the dogs and once without." She looked at Raina. "Does that sound familiar?"

The other girl shrugged. "I don't know. I don't look people in the eye that much. Part of me is still embarrassed to be out here."

After a moment's hesitation, Alexis said, "So why are you out here? If it's okay to ask."

"It's okay." Raina lifted one hand. "I had a big fight with my mom, and I ran away. Our house is too crowded. I have to share a room with three of my sisters, and there's not enough money. But now I realize that I was stupid."

"Why don't you go back?"

Raina shrugged. "I'm proud. And"—she hesitated—"I'm afraid she'll say no. It's only been three months, but it feels like three years. The other night, one of the workers gave me a towel fresh out of the dryer for my shower." Smiling, she hugged herself. "The feeling of wrapping up in a hot towel was amazing. I miss so many things I never thought twice about before."

"Like what?"

Raina stopped so she could give the answer her full concentration. "Like everything. Like pillows, fuzzy blankets, stuffed animals, hot cocoa, my bed, clean socks, hair straighteners, and curling irons. Being able to do laundry whenever I want. It's pretty useless to shower and then put on dirty clothes. Oh, and the edge of the bathtub so I can put my leg up and shave. Being able to sit down or lie down without people giving me dirty looks."

"Why don't you try calling your mom?" Alexis ventured. "What's the worst that could happen? Even if she said no, it wouldn't be any worse than it is now."

"Oh, yes it would be," Raina said fiercely. "If I don't call, I can still have hope that she'll say yes." She raised her dark eyes to Alexis's face. "And if she says no, then that's it. That's the end."

"But nothing's ever really the end, though," Alexis said. "Things change. Even people change."

"Maybe," Raina said, not sounding like she believed it.

She caught sight of a clock on the outside of a bank. "Hey, I've got to go meet my caseworker now. Will you be okay on your own?"

Alexis nodded, suddenly feeling ashamed of how she was pretending. Even though her motivation was different, was she any better than Miranda? She took out her phone. "Give me your phone number, and I'll text you later, okay?"

Raina bit her lip and looked away. "I don't have a phone anymore."

"Oh," Alexis said. "Then will I see you around?"

"Oh, I'm sure you will. If not today, then soon. Portland isn't that big."

They exchanged smiles and then Raina folded her into a quick, hard hug. Alexis was starting to put her phone back in her pocket when she saw that Ruby had texted her. Half a dozen times. First about Tiffany Yee's death. Then about how she had been grounded and her parents were forcing to her to leave SAR. Alexis winced. She might not really understand how Ruby's mind worked, but she knew one thing: SAR was the best thing that had ever happened to the girl.

The next text from Ruby begged Alexis to go with Nick in Ruby's stead tomorrow. With Tiffany Yee's death, she said, it was imperative that they figure out who the runner was. Alexis texted Ruby and Nick that she would take Ruby's place.

She spent the rest of the morning asking about her mom, again with no success. At noon, she went to the Park Blocks, where she had heard that a church was serving up a weekly lunch. Her mouth watering, she showed her mom's photo to everyone in line, with no success. The food was heaped in clear plastic tubs like the ones where her mom kept her scrapbooking supplies. There was no place to sit, so Alexis stood hunched over a plate of stew ladled onto mashed potatoes, enjoying every warm, steamy bite.

"Hey, darlin'," a man's voice drawled. Alexis looked up—and froze. It was the homeless guy she, Nick, and Ruby had talked to on the trail shortly before they found Miranda's body. He was smiling at her appreciatively, and she could tell he had no idea they had met before. Of course, dressed in her mom's shapeless clothes and with her hair finger-combed, Alexis looked nothing like the earnest young volunteer who had worn a red climbing helmet, a blue Gore-Tex jacket, and an orange waterproof cover over her SAR backpack.

"Um, hi," she said, her voice betraying her uncertainty. Normally she wouldn't even look at anyone who talked to her like that. But Detective Harriman had told her they hadn't been able to find the homeless guy.

With a grin, he moved a little closer, close enough that she could hear the skull-shaped beads on the ends of his dreads tapping against each other. "After you're done eating, want to go someplace?" He tapped his pocket meaningfully and raised an eyebrow. "Maybe have a little party?"

Alexis froze. Had he said those same words to Miranda and Tiffany and the third dead girl? From what she knew about the first two girls, those words might have been enough to have them agree.

Alexis had to alert Detective Harriman. "Sure." She forced her lips into a smile she hoped looked genuine. "Let me just go to the bathroom first."

HAD TO HAVE IT

FOR THE LAST TWO DAYS, RUBY HAD DONE exactly what her parents had ordered her to do. More or less. She had only left the house to go to school and come straight home. While her parents were at work, they called every hour to make sure she was staying put. Because her dad still had her cell phone, she hadn't been able to call or text anyone on it. But that hadn't stopped Ruby from using the house phone and texting on her computer. She was pretty sure her parents didn't even know it was possible to text from a computer, but she wasn't about to ask.

When her parents had come home from work Monday, they had found her curled on her bed in the dark, her fingers running ceaselessly back and forth over the satin binding on her blanket. It was a habit that dated back to when she was an infant, according to her parents, and one she still retreated to in times of great stress. When they asked her questions, she answered with just a word or two. She refused dinner, saying only "not hungry" and turning away from the light. Her parents talked to her and to each other in low voices, like she was sick.

Ruby was sick, sick with longing for SAR. Her parents didn't understand how important it was to her. There was very little about her that they did understand. But Clinically Depressed Daughter they might get, so Ruby had decided to take all of her feelings and reactions and make them bigger than life. This morning they had insisted she go to school, then shot worried looks at each other when she ate only two bites of cereal.

But underneath her passive exterior, no matter what she was doing—lying in bed, riding the bus, sitting in class—Ruby was consumed with solving the mystery. Why had the killer targeted Miranda, Tiffany, and the still nameless girl? Why these three particular girls? Three girls. Three different races. One a poor student and rich. One a good student and poor. And one a question mark. All of them homeless or pretending to be.

If she knew the why, it could tell her the who. Was it the homeless guy? He had flirted with Alexis yesterday, offered her drugs. But when Alexis had tried to stall him long enough to call Detective Harriman, he had slipped away. A homeless guy might have different reasons for targeting homeless girls than someone who lived a more "normal" life.

And there was the runner that Alexis and Nick were going to try to track down tonight. The one Alexis had seen arguing with another girl who looked homeless. If he was the killer, it was even possible that the girl with the tiny blue stars tattooed on her face was already dead, just waiting for someone to find her body.

Why had the killer chosen these three—or four—girls to strangle? It had to be more than just homelessness. There were dozens and dozens of homeless girls and women in Portland, drawn by the mild climate, the number of social service agencies, and the fairly laid-back attitude. So if you had been driven to kill a black homeless girl because she reminded you of, say, your first girlfriend, you could easily find even more black homeless girls to kill. But instead the killer's next victim had been a white girl who only pretended to be homeless. And instead of targeting a black or white girl after that, the killer had next strangled an Asian-American girl.

Now as she walked back to her house from the bus stop, Ruby replayed the conversation she had had after school yesterday with Nick about Tiffany Yee. She had called him on the house phone.

"But Tiffany Yee doesn't look anything like Miranda Wyatt or that other girl who died," he had said. "And you said serial killers have a type. What kind of serial killer murders girls who aren't anything alike?"

Nick had a point, Ruby thought as she stepped into the living room and the alarm panel next to the door began to beep. In the dimness, her mom's collection of owls stared at her. Plush, ceramic, or wooden. Crouching, proud, or wings spread. Realistic, primitive, or cartoonlike. With eyes made of buttons, paint, or glittering rhinestones.

Her dad was always after her mom to stop buying them, but if she saw one she didn't have—an owl wearing a graduation cap, or a set of owl-shaped salt and pepper shakers, or a paperweight carved to look like an owl— then it was like she *had* to have it.

Behind Ruby, the alarm began to beep faster and faster. But she didn't hear it.

Because suddenly the pieces of the puzzle came together.

COLLECT THE WHOLE SET

"I'VE FIGURED IT OUT," A GIRL'S VOICE SAID as soon as Alexis pulled her cell phone from her pocket and said hello. Last night, defeated, she had finally returned to the apartment. It was clear that her mother hadn't been home in her absence. Bran had texted her several times. Not wanting to lie and not wanting to tell the truth, she had just texted back that she was really busy and would talk to him later. This morning, she had gone back to school. She had barely heard a word her teachers said, her mind preoccupied by the problem of what she was going to do if her mom never came home. But she had still been able to hope. She'd even hurried home from school, imagining that her mom might be there.

Alexis was standing in the empty rooms, feeling disappointment settle onto her like a weight, when the phone rang.

"I know why those girls died. And I know who he's going to kill next," the girl continued.

"Ruby?" For a second, Alexis stopped thinking about her mom. "Is that you?"

"Serial killers always have a type."

Something Ruby had already said. More than once. "Yes," Alexis agreed impatiently.

"So why would he choose one black, one white, and one Asian?" Ruby didn't pause for an answer. "Alexis, he's collecting them!"

"Collecting them?" She wasn't following.

"You know how they say on commercials, 'Collect the whole set'? That's just what this guy is doing."

Alexis no longer saw her empty apartment. She thought of the nameless girl in the newspaper article, Miranda's half-open eye, Tiffany's photo on the memorial wall. "So you're saying that's the point? That's why they don't look anything alike?"

"Exactly. He wants one of each."

"One of each? So who's next?" Alexis thought of the dead girls. Black, white, Asian. She answered her own question. "He'll go for a Hispanic girl." She thought of the dark-haired girl at the bus mall with the tattoos on her face. "That girl I saw the runner arguing with—she could have been Hispanic."

At the other end of the line, Ruby sucked in her breath. "That's why you and Nick have to figure out who the runner is tonight. And then we'll go back to Harriman."

Alexis had called the detective yesterday, told him that the homeless guy with the dreads had offered to party with her. But she had felt compelled to leave out a few facts that would have made the story more interesting, like the fact that she was pretending to be homeless. Harriman had sounded distracted and uninterested.

"Okay. But there's something else I have to do first." She pictured Raina sprawled under a tree, a red line around her neck, her body growing cold, one eye not quite closed.

Alexis couldn't let that happen.

THE SILVER TRACKS OF HER TEARS

NICK SCANNED THE TRAIL, KEEPING EYES and ears alert for the first sign of the runner. Was this what it had been like for his dad in Iraq when he was out on a mission? He imagined an enemy soldier creeping silently toward him.

Nick had been so excited that he had come here straight after school, long before Alexis arrived. She had only shown up a few minutes ago. With reddened eyes, she had talked about a homeless Hispanic girl she knew. A girl she now couldn't find. Normally Nick would have loved to have her spilling her guts to him, but he knew they had to get into position. Five minutes ago, Nick had finally insisted they go to their hiding spots.

And now Nick heard noises. Feet slapped down the path. A body pushed through brush. He sucked in his breath and tried to hold absolutely still.

It was only when a dog crashed into his legs that he realized they had forgotten to account for the animals. Both of them now nosed Nick's crotch and whined while he tried to silently shoo them away, pushing their heads.

Why was he stuck with both of them? Alexis was a couple hundred yards back on the trail, so why wasn't at least one of them bugging her?

The man whistled as he ran past. "Leave it, Milly, Murphy! Leave it!"

With one last sniff, the dogs took off after the runner.

Nick waited a half minute and then followed. A hundred yards farther on, the trail turned. He couldn't see the guy. He couldn't see the dogs. He could hear them, though, and he was a fast runner. Nick imagined himself an Indian scout, one with nature, able to run silently through the forest for miles. He even leapt over a log. But when he rounded the bend, there was still no sign of anyone, man or beast. Nick put the power on, his backpack thumping with each step, ignoring the fact that his side was starting to feel like someone had stabbed him and left the knife behind.

Finally he reached the edge of the parking lot. He ducked behind a tree. The runner had taken the leashes from his pocket—the same leashes he had probably strangled those girls with—and was clipping them on the dogs. When Alexis came huffing up behind Nick, he turned with his finger on his lips. "He's just putting leashes on them. He hasn't gone near a car. I think he might have walked here."

Which was good, because it meant they didn't have to try to get close enough to read his license plate. When the runner left the parking lot, they fell into step behind him, keeping about a block back.

But what if the guy looked back? Nick grabbed Alexis's hand.

"What are you doing?" she hissed, trying to yank it back. One of the dogs lifted its head.

"Pretending we're a couple," he said out of the side of his mouth. Despite everything that was happening, he felt a secret thrill saying the word. "He's not going to be worried about a couple following him."

"Oh." Alexis stopped trying to pull away, but her hand was still a tight knot in his.

After a few blocks, the runner turned up a walkway in front of a house. It was situated on a corner lot, set well away from its neighbors. Nick looked back. They were only five or six blocks from the border of Forest Park. Easy access for anyone who needed to dump a body. A shiver ran over him.

The man unlocked the front door, then unclipped the dogs from their leashes. The dogs bounded into the darkened house ahead of him. Then he went inside and the living room light came on. Alexis ducked behind a telephone pole across the street, and Nick tucked himself in behind her. Through the open blinds, they watched him move through the living room until he turned right and disappeared down what must be a hall.

At the far end of the house, a light came on. Through white lace curtains, they saw a tall figure entering the room and a shorter, slighter one getting off a bed. The shorter one raised its hands in front of its face, as if warding off a blow. Nick sucked in his breath. The tall one was definitely the runner. But the other, the shorter and slighter one? Nick was pretty sure it was a girl. A dark-haired girl. His heart was beating like a crazy windup toy.

The guy was waving his arms, and even from across the street, they could hear the faint sounds of yelling as he moved toward the girl.

As the guy got closer to her and farther away from the door, the girl suddenly ducked under his arm and made a run for it. First out of the room, and then a second later, the front door of the house flew open and she came barreling out. Her eyes were wild, and her feet were bare.

Nick and Alexis didn't have time to move or even breathe before the man appeared, scrambling down the steps after the girl. He lunged forward and grabbed her wrist. He yanked her so hard she stumbled backward.

"No!" she screamed. "No, you can't do this to me! No!"

He didn't answer. He just dragged her back up the stairs, forced her inside, and slammed the door shut.

Wide-eyed, Alexis and Nick stared at each other.

"Is that the girl you know?"

She shook her head. "But I think it's the one I saw him with at the bus stop."

"Crap!" Nick thought he was going to throw up. "He's probably killing her right now!"

Alexis was already dialing 9-1-1. In a high-pitched voice, she told the dispatcher to send the police and gave them the address of the house. "A man's holding a girl captive there, and I think he's trying to kill her." Her voice sharpened with urgency. "She just tried to get away, and he dragged her back inside." After a pause, Alexis put her hand over the mouthpiece. "They have units on the way."

The cops might be coming, but would they be fast enough? Hadn't Ruby told them that if someone strangled you, you could die in ninety seconds?

But that wasn't going to happen now. Not to another girl. Not if Nick had anything to say about it.

"We've got to stop him," he said. He didn't know who he was talking to and then he realized it was himself. "We can't let him kill another girl." He slipped his backpack off one shoulder and blindly yanked out a notebook.

"What are you doing?" Alexis said.

Instead of answering, Nick let the backpack thump to the ground and pounded across the street. He took the two steps in a single bound, his finger already jabbing the button for the doorbell. He had never been more frightened in his life.

Inside, the bell echoed. Nick held his breath. No answering voice. No footsteps. Not even a whisper.

He leaned on the button until it let out a continuous peal.

The runner wrenched open the door. "What?" he snarled. His face was flushed, contorted with anger.

Think, Nick, think! He pasted the world's fakest smile on his face, and suddenly the words just came to him. "Good evening. Um, I'm going door-to-door today on behalf of Ruby McClure, your independent candidate for mayor." He flipped open his notebook, which was filled with his biology notes. Hopefully this guy couldn't read his bad handwriting upside down. A lightning bolt of panic shot through Nick as he realized he didn't even have a pen. Still he poised his empty hand over the page as if he were holding one. "So how do you intend to vote?"

The guy stared at him. "Are you talking about the election?"

"Um, yes." His ears strained to hear the girl, but behind the man the house was silent. Silent as a grave. *Please,* Nick prayed, *please let her be okay.*

"The election was over a week ago."

Obviously he should have paid more attention in social studies. "We're getting a head start on the next one."

The man's eyes narrowed. "Do I know you?"

Widening his eyes, Nick tried to look innocent. "I don't think so." This angry-looking man bore little resemblance to the happy-go-lucky runner with two dogs he had met a week ago. Nick hoped that, minus his SAR gear, the same was true for him.

From farther back in the house came a noise. Nick held his breath. It sounded like whimpering. His blood turned to ice. He scanned the man's empty hands, checked his waistband for the bulge of a gun. He was taller and heavier than Nick, and from what they had just seen on the trail, faster. But at least Nick couldn't see any weapons.

"Wait a second," the man said. "Do you know Mallory?"

That must be the name of the girl he was holding captive. The one who was whimpering from whatever he had done to her. But what was the right answer?

The right answer, Nick figured, would be whatever kept the guy talking to him. Because as long as he was talking to him, he couldn't be hurting the girl any further.

"I do know Mallory." He took a deep breath "And you can't get away with what you're doing."

"Oh, no?" The runner took a step forward so the two of them were chest to chest. "You don't understand how things work. I'm the one who makes the rules here. I suggest you shut your mouth and leave right now."

"Or what?" Nick managed to say with a tongue that was suddenly as dry as a desert.

"Or I'll be forced to do something neither of us will like very much."

Out of the corner of his eye, Nick saw the man's right hand begin to rise, the fingers curling into a fist.

It seemed like a good idea to duck, so with a sudden lurch, he did. But they were standing so close that his temple smacked right into the middle of the guy's face. He felt the man's nose give with a sickening crack.

With a shout, the guy staggered backward, blood fountaining from his nose. He put his hands up and pulled them back, staring at the bright crimson with mingled amazement and anger.

"You broke my nose!" he said as he grabbed the shoulders of Nick's jacket.

And just at that moment, three police cars converged on the house, their red and blue lights splitting the night, their sirens deafening. In seconds, officers were out and crouched behind their doors, guns drawn, yelling orders.

A minute later, both Nick and the runner were on their knees on the sharp gravel of the driveway, their hands laced behind their heads. Blood was still dripping from the man's nose. An unmarked car pulled up, lights flashing in the grille, and Detective Harriman got out.

Alexis hurried up to him and began to explain. "That guy's the one who did it." She pointed. "The runner we saw that day. He's the real killer. He must have strangled them with his dog's leash. And there's a girl in the house that he's holding captive."

"I don't know who in the hell this chick is," the runner said, his voice oddly nasal because of his broken nose, "but she's crazy. Don't listen to her."

But Detective Harriman did. "Captive?" he echoed as he drew his gun. He quickly conferred with a couple of cops and then the three of them went in the house together, guns pointed into the darkness as the men darted around corners and leapfrogged each other.

Nick's heart was pounding in his ears. What would they find? Was the girl even still alive?

A few minutes later, the cops came outside with her. Nick was relieved to see that she was walking under her own power. It was full dark now, but even in the shadows, he could see the silver tracks of her tears.

The girl—Mallory?—was alive. Alive, and as far as Nick could see, uninjured, although she was shivering and hugging herself. Nick could breathe again. She was alive and safe. One of the cops shrugged out of his jacket and draped it over her shoulders. Suddenly she spun away from him, darted over to the runner, and slapped him across the face. And then the cops were pulling her off as she screamed insults at him.

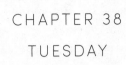

OBSERVATIONS YOU MISSED

FROM THE INTRODUCTION TO *A BIRDING JOURNAL:*

USING YOUR JOURNAL

Take notes on what the specimen was doing as you observed it. Record general behaviors and specific reactions to new events, such as the appearance of a predator or how it interacts with others. Note large actions such as preening, flight patterns, and foraging habits, as well as small movements such as tail bobs, head cocks, or wing stretches.

Record the specimen's appearance, including the brilliance of plumage, any peculiar markings, and any remarkable or unusual features such as missing feathers or signs of illness.

To make the most of your journal, review it regularly. Studying your notes can help you see what observations you missed so you will know what to look for the next time you see a bird. Comparing your notes on similar specimens can help you learn to accurately identify them, and over time you will learn more than you've ever dreamed.

Your detailed notes can be a way to enjoy sightings over and over as you study your observations and remember exactly the circumstances of each sighting and what made it special.

SPECIES NAME
Homeless, also known as street people, hobos, bums, drifters.

INDIVIDUAL SPECIMEN
Tiffany Yee, aged 17.

STUDY SPECIFICATIONS
This 17-year-old female, who had been homeless for approximately eight weeks, had a tracking program covertly installed on her cell phone on November 1 and was then returned to the study area in downtown Portland, Oregon. Her movements and daily activity were monitored until November 12, using GPS coordinates provided by the tracking program. Once her position had been determined, it was possible, on a few occasions, to take advantage of topography and surreptitiously photograph her.

For the purpose of moving her, the subject was immobilized with gamma-hydroxybutyric acid administered orally in Kahlua and cream. Once study was completed, subject was euthanized.

STUDY FINDINGS:
APPEARANCE
Approximately five foot five, 130 pounds. Chinese-American, with light brown skin. Hair straight,

approximately 33 cm in length, a beautiful glossy black. Typically dressed in jeans, black boots, and either a red sweater or a gray turtleneck under a black North Face hip-length coat. Carried belongings in a pink Hello Kitty! backpack. Despite poor diet, appeared healthy, except for occasional bouts of coughing.

HABITAT

Nocturnal: Spent nights at Outside In, Porch Light Shelter, the Red Cross Warming Center, the bottom level of a parking garage on Fourth Avenue, and occasionally in parked cars or men's homes. The proportion of time that subject was active in the middle of the night was inversely correlated with the nightly minimum temperature.

Diurnal: Spent days walking in downtown Portland, with occasional forays into Portland County Library, McDonald's, and Pioneer Courthouse Square.

FEEDING HABITS

Most meals provided by service agencies. When left to own devices, preferred high-fat, high-salt, high-starch foods such as bread, potato chips, cookie dough, and French fries. Used a variety of illegal drugs as well as cigarettes and alcohol.

BEHAVIOR

When not sleeping at a shelter, did not congregate with other homeless on a regular basis. Frequently

spent time at Portland County Library, especially
when daytime temperature dropped below 40. Had
a distinctive walk, fast, with head down, not
making eye contact. Occasionally panhandled, stole
unattended items, or broke into cars to steal small
electronics and/or sleep.

VOCALIZATION
Quiet, soft-spoken, with good vocabulary.

———

SPECIES NAME
Teenager.

INDIVIDUAL SPECIMEN
Ruby McClure, age 16.

STUDY SPECIFICATIONS
This 16-year-old female was first observed on
November 8. Her movements and daily activity have
been monitored since November 13, using GPS
coordinates provided by the tracking program
incorporated in a unit disguised as a thumb drive
and hidden in subject's backpack.

STUDY FINDINGS:
APPEARANCE
Approximately five foot four, 120 pounds, Caucasian
with milk-white skin. Hair is straight, approximately
60 cm in length, and an unusual and striking
true red. Dresses plainly and practically in

neutral-colored sweaters, jeans, Nikes, and a navy blue parka.

HABITAT
Nocturnal: Spends nights at familial home on NW Pettygrove.

Diurnal: Weekdays are spent at Lincoln High School. Evenings and weekends are often dedicated to outings or classes with Portland County Search and Rescue in a three-county area.

FEEDING HABITS
Healthy diet. Is almost always chewing gum.

BEHAVIOR
Awkward, intense, fixated on certain topics. Does not make much eye contact.

VOCALIZATION
Can be loud and insistent when interested in topic.

CRY FOR ALL
THE GIRLS

THEY HAD DONE IT! SHE AND NICK HAD caught the killer and saved a girl! Even Detective Harriman had gruffly thanked them—before lecturing them about the importance of leaving things to the professionals. Then the police had briefly questioned both of them and taken them home.

Alexis should have been relieved, even happy, as she walked up the stairs to her apartment. But she just felt shaky and empty. The adrenaline had worn off, and now she barely had the energy to lift her feet. Even though they might have saved future homeless girls and women, her mom was still missing. Maybe dead. She hadn't even been able to find Raina before she met Nick in Forest Park. Who knew how many bodies the runner was responsible for?

Alexis couldn't think of anywhere else to look for her mom, any other way to find her. What if her mom never came back? Could she make it on her own?

In the short term, the answer to that was easy. She had been forging her mom's signature on the disability check for years, just as she had been forging it on any-thing else important, like the application for SAR.

But eventually some adult was going to figure out that Alexis was alone, and then what?

She let herself into the apartment, so lost in thought that at first she didn't realize someone was already there. But a tall, thin figure was standing in the kitchen.

"Mommy?" Alexis said in a voice so high-pitched and soft even she didn't recognize it.

Her mom turned and smiled. "Oh, honey, you're home."

Alexis couldn't speak. Instead she wrapped her arms around her mom so tight they both lost their balance and bumped into the counter. She pressed her nose against her mom's neck. It had been months, maybe even years, since Alexis had held her mom so close, but she almost couldn't believe that she was real. That she was alive.

Finally she pulled back. "Where *were* you?"

Her mom smiled ruefully. "I got picked up because the cops thought I was drunk. I don't really remember much about what happened next, but I guess they decided I wasn't drunk, I was crazy. So I ended up in a locked hos-pital ward while they evaluated me. But they can only hold you so long, and I wasn't about to let them put me away. Not when I needed to get back to my baby girl. So I was as sly as a fox." She grinned and laid her finger against her lips. "I knew they might take you away if I whispered one word about you, so I kept quiet."

Her mom was back. Her real mom. In spirit as well as body. On her feet were cheap white tennis shoes, and she was dressed in purple sweatpants and a gray sweatshirt that hung on her skinny frame. Her nails were clean and short. Her eyes clear. But a tic flicked underneath her left eye, and she kept smacking her lips.

"So you're taking your meds again, Mom?"

"They gave me a lot of pills. A lot. Some of them new." She pointed at a crumpled brown paper bag.

Alexis opened it. It was full of paperwork and pill bottles. Even more pills than her mom normally took. Drugs for depression, for anxiety, for delusions, for insomnia. Some you took with food, some you took on an empty stomach. All of them had to be taken at set intervals, although some couldn't be taken together. How her mom was supposed to continue on this regimen without someone to supervise it was beyond Alexis. And that assumed she continued to be willing to take them at all.

Her mom licked her lips again and then opened her mouth, revealing thick ropes of saliva. "You know I don't like the way they make me feel. So slow. Slow and tired."

"But you have to take them, Mom. You have to. Promise me. Because"—Alexis's voice broke—"because I can't be on my own like that again. I can't. Not knowing where you are! Thinking you might be dead!"

The events of the last few days caught up with her. Her legs felt shaky. She sat down on the couch, put her head in her hands, and started to cry. Cry for all the girls and women they hadn't saved.

And a few tears for herself.

LIFE LIST

THE HOUSE PHONE WAS RINGING WHEN Ruby got home from school. She had been distracted all day, thinking about how Alexis and Nick had caught the runner and saved the girl. Her only regret was that she hadn't been there. Last night, she had barely slept. Once her parents were in bed, she kept checking websites, waiting for the story to go live. But so far, the police were keeping a lid on it.

When Ruby answered the phone, it was her mom.

"Your father and I just met with that Jon Partridge. From Search and Rescue. When we called to tell him we were pulling you out, he asked if we could talk."

"Yes?" Ruby said slowly, not daring to let herself hope.

"He told us that you've been acing all your tests. And he said you're becoming a real asset to SAR." Her mom's voice was filled with some emotion Ruby couldn't name. Was it—pride? "He said you actually stopped one of the other volunteers from touching some important evidence. And he said they needed you."

"Uh-huh." This wasn't news to Ruby, but it clearly was to her mom.

"He also said volunteering for SAR was excellent preparation for being a doctor, especially working in emergency medicine."

"I think I would be good at that," Ruby said. It was 100 percent true. She pressed her lips together so she didn't add that she had also decided it was not what she wanted to do.

"So we worked out an agreement. SAR won't call you in if they're recovering the body of a murder victim or even looking for crime scene evidence if it's gruesome in any way. You're only sixteen. We don't want you exposed to things like that."

"Okay," Ruby said slowly. *Was her mom saying . . . ?*

"And you have to clear it with us if you're asked to leave school."

"Okay." She was nodding her head as if her mom could see her.

"And we can change our minds at any time if we feel you're getting too obsessed."

"Okay."

"Aren't you happy, Ruby?" her mom said, and only then was Ruby certain she was back in SAR.

"It's what I want most in the world." Emotion thickened her voice. "Thank you. I won't let you and Dad down."

"We just want you to be happy, Ruby. Happy and healthy."

"So can I go to class tonight?"

Her mom sighed. "Your keys and cell phone are in my underwear drawer."

"Is it okay if I leave a little early?"

"Why?" Her mom drew out the word, as if she were suspicious.

"Because the swifts are back at Chapman, and I want to go see them."

Her mom let out a laugh. "Of course, honey. Enjoy."

Ruby ran to get her cell phone so she could tell Alexis and Nick the good news.

It was just an hour until sunset, when the swifts would roost. Every space along Northwest Portland's narrow streets was taken. Cars were even parked in loading zones and in front of driveways.

"This had better be worth it," Nick said as Ruby drove in ever-widening circles, trying to find a parking space. "Because we are going to have quite a hike."

"It might be the last chance to see them. Ever," Ruby said. "Since they're so late this year, who knows if they'll come again? So this might be your once-in-a-lifetime chance." It had been a shock to learn that neither Nick nor Alexis had ever come here to watch the swifts. She finally spotted a tiny parking space and backed expertly into it, ignoring the honks of the car behind her. They were actually closer to Forest Park than to Chapman Elementary.

Nick was still complaining as they got out of the car. Then he tipped his head back and his mouth fell open. The sky overhead was thick with birds, swirling like innumerable flecks of black pepper. "There must be hundreds," Nick said. "Thousands."

"At least," Ruby agreed. "Chapman is one of the largest known roosting sites."

They joined the crowds on the sidewalk walking toward the school grounds. Ruby was used to seeing pedestrians looking down, distracted by their smart phones. It was weird to see so many people nearly running into telephone poles, signs, and each other because they were looking *up*. All of them taking in the spectacle of the dark whirling clouds of birds.

"Have you seen that movie *The Birds*?" Nick asked. His shoulders hunched as if he expected an imminent attack. "They wouldn't hurt us, would they?"

"That was a *movie*." Ruby tried not to sound impatient. Next he would be asking her if zombies were real. "A movie based on a short story, except all Hitchcock took from it was the idea of birds attacking people. Don't worry. The birds have a lot more to fear from us than we do from them. In fact, we're the ones who've destroyed their habitat and made the world so hot, which is what is probably screwing up their migration." She thought of a joke. "If they ever did turn on us, you could say it was the swifts coming home to roost. Get it? Like when they say the chickens come home to roost?"

"Ha ha," Nick said, but Ruby wasn't certain he really thought it was funny.

Hundreds of people were gathered on the school grounds. Some stood, others sat on camp chairs or folding aluminum lawn chairs. A few families had spread out blankets and were picnicking despite how cold the ground must be. All of them had their heads tilted back, their faces lit by the salmon-colored glow of the setting sun. People pointed fingers and cameras. Kids chased each other through the crowd. Dogs on leashes barked.

As the birds continued to gather overhead like iron filings swirling around a magnet, Ruby and Nick hunted through the crowd for Alexis. After watching the swifts, they would go to the sheriff's office for class. They finally found her standing by the swing sets. She hugged Nick. Then, to Ruby's surprise and delight, she turned and hugged her.

"I'm so proud of both of you guys for catching the killer!" Ruby grinned at them, feeling almost giddy.

"All I did was call 9-1-1 and Detective Harriman," Alexis said. "Nick's the one who broke that guy's nose. Just straight-up head-butted him."

"And what about you, Ruby?" Nick said. "You're the one who knew Adams didn't kill Miranda. You're the one who realized how those three dead girls were connected. And you're the one who figured out how to find the real killer." He turned to Alexis. "And if you hadn't spotted the runner with that girl downtown, Ruby might not have been able to put everything together." He grinned. "I think Detective Harriman might owe us a medal. Or three."

"Yeah, that sounds *exactly* like the kind of guy he is," Alexis said. She put on an exaggerated frown as she tilted her head back and looked down her nose at them. "Now, don't you go thinking you're some kind of heroes," she said in a gravelly voice, "because you're not."

It was a pretty good imitation of the detective. Ruby laughed along with Nick, although she felt a little disloyal. After all, Detective Harriman *had* come when Alexis called.

Ruby asked, "So have you guys talked to him since last night?"

Nick shook his head. "We still haven't been called back in."

From behind them, a man's voice said, "Enjoying the show?" It was the bird-watcher, the one who looked like Santa Claus. Caleb Becker. His binoculars were around his neck, and a big silver thermos was tucked under his arm.

"I'm glad they came back," Ruby said. "Thank you so much for telling me about it."

"You guys want some cocoa to celebrate?" He pulled a short stack of paper cups from the patch pocket of his coat.

"Sure," Alexis said with a little shiver. "It's cold tonight."

"But clear," Becker said as he poured cocoa for Alexis and then Nick. "Perfect weather for bird-watching. After the swifts roost, I'm going to head over to Forest Park. I'm hoping I'll get lucky and get a peek at that northern spotted owl." He fumbled a little with Ruby's cup before handing it over and then tapped his own paper cup against hers. "To life lists," he said, making a little birding joke.

"To life lists," she echoed, and then raised the cup to her lips. It tasted like instant cocoa, not so much of chocolate as of chemicals and salt and artificial sweetener. Ruby drank it down fast, to be polite, the way her parents had taught her to deal with food she didn't like. Since Becker was watching, she tried not to make a face.

Around them, people began to call out and point. "There they go!" a man shouted. The birds were starting to funnel into the chimney, a black tornado of tiny flying bodies.

Ruby's phone rang. She pulled it from her coat pocket. "Hello?" A few of the watchers turned to glare at her. She started moving to the edge of the crowd so she wouldn't disturb them.

"Ruby McClure?" a gruff voice asked.

"Yes." She drew the word out hesitantly.

"You kids need to stay away from my case." It was Detective Harriman.

And she was pretty sure he sounded angry.

SO-CALLED KILLER

"WHAT'S WRONG?" RUBY ASKED.

"You got those other two riled up," Detective Harriman said, "thinking they were supposed to be doing my job or something. Only you're not a detective, you're not a cop, you're not a superhero. So don't go acting like one. I don't need you guys messing things up again like you did last night."

"What are you talking about?" Ruby had reached the now-empty sidewalk.

"That guy you told Alexis and Nick was the killer?" His voice rose. "The one they followed and assaulted?"

"Wait—isn't he?" Ruby braced herself against a telephone pole as a wave of dizziness washed over her. Even though she was standing still, she felt as if she were moving. Or maybe the world was moving around her.

"Of course not. Your so-called killer is actually a dad. A dad who didn't want to let his teenage daughter go out partying. He wasn't holding her captive. She was grounded." The detective took a ragged breath, let it out. "You keep seeing one and one and trying to add them up to eleven. So thanks to interference from you and your friends, I ended up dragging some innocent guy downtown for questioning, and I came out looking like an idiot. We'll be lucky if he doesn't sue us for false imprisonment."

Ruby's stomach did a slow flip. "Then who killed those girls?"

"Don't you understand?" Harriman's voice was tight with anger. "Adams killed Miranda Wyatt, and we don't know yet who killed the other two. It's probably not even the same guy. There is nothing to link them. No DNA evidence. No fingerprints. The two don't even look anything alike."

Ruby's dizziness was getting worse. She tried closing her eyes, then opening them. It didn't help. "Even though they didn't look alike, they still could have been killed by the same guy. I've been thinking about it." It was getting harder to make one word follow another in a logical fashion. Harder to care about what she was saying, although some buried part of her knew she should. "What if they're all different because that's what he's looking for? Black, white, Asian? What if he wants one of each? What if he's collecting them? You need to find that homeless guy and question him."

"Oh, good grief." Detective Harriman exhaled heavily. "Stop. Just stop. That's enough. Don't try and say that because there's no pattern, it means there really *is* one. I'm telling you now, and I'm going to tell Nick and Alexis—you guys need to leave the police work to the police." And with a click, he was gone.

Ruby shook her head and then was sorry she had. It

felt like her brain was sloshing back and forth in her skull. Maybe watching all those whirling birds had given her vertigo. *Vertigo.* Like *The Birds*, it was the name of an Alfred Hitchcock movie. She found herself smiling, and then the smile faded away as she lost track of the thought.

"Everything okay?"

She turned. It was Becker, his face creased with concern.

"I feel kind of dizzy."

"Here. Let's get away from the crowd." He put one hand under her elbow and began to guide her. "Get you some fresh air."

That seemed like a good idea. A great idea, in fact. "That might help." Ruby let him lead her, grateful to put herself in someone else's care. It was taking all her concentration to put one foot in front of the other. Her body felt loose and tingly, but her face was on fire. She put her free hand to her forehead and pressed on it, trying to cool it off. Her face felt weird. She pinched her cheek. It was numb.

She and Becker were alone on the street, everyone still back at the school, staring up at the sky. "I'm so glad the swifts came back," she said. Her voice seemed to echo along the empty row of houses. "Am I too loud? Am I talking too loud?"

"You're fine, Ruby." He smiled down at her. "You're just perfect."

Her head was a balloon, and her feet didn't belong to her. "That's nice of you to say that, but I know that people generally don't like me." She gave voice to what she normally only thought. "I know I'm different. I can't help it. I don't even know what normal is. Just that I'm not."

"Normal is overrated. Who wants to be normal, to be average?" He snorted and shook his head. "Wouldn't you rather be special?"

Could he be right? Something about his words resonated with her. She nodded in agreement, and then realized she needed to stop.

She looked around. "I should probably get back. I need to take Alexis and Nick to the sheriff's office."

"Why don't we see if we can find that spotted owl first?" Becker suggested. "It's not very far from here. It should only take a moment. And then you'll have it for your life list, too."

"Okay!" Ruby imagined the gray bird turning its pale face, shaped like an English walnut, toward them. Nature was amazing. The swifts, the rising moon, and now the promise of a spotted owl. Her thoughts were a jumble of images.

They started up the hill to Forest Park. There was no sidewalk here, just a stretch of muddy ground. Ruby fell into step behind Becker. They were leaving their footprints behind just as their shoes were picking up some of the mud. Locard's principle of exchange. Ruby was pleased that she remembered the name. Locard. She murmured it to herself, rolling the *r*. It was so musical.

"Did you say something?" Becker looked back over his shoulder.

"Not really." She stretched out her arms for balance, smiling to herself, thinking *Locarda, Locardee, Locardi, Locardo*. Becker's boots were leaving a pattern of diamond and chevron shapes. A pattern Ruby had seen before, although she couldn't quite remember where. Blinking, she stopped and tried to focus. Why was it so familiar?

And then it came to her.

She had seen that same pattern in the shoe print left next to the body of Miranda Wyatt.

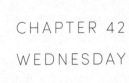

WITHOUT EVEN SAYING GOOD-BYE

NICK HAD WATCHED AS ALEXIS'S FACE WENT white after she answered her phone. She had said only yes and no, and once a "no, sir." He had been opening his mouth to ask what was wrong when his own phone rang. It was Detective Harriman, and when he was finished with Nick, he hung up without even saying good-bye. Nick guessed that if Harriman had been on a landline, he would have crashed the receiver down. But since it was a cell phone, all it made was a quiet click.

Swearing, Nick took the phone away from his ear and hit the END button. Alexis shook her head. They were the only ones not staring at the spectacle in the sky.

"I assume you got the lecture, too?" she asked.

"Yeah." Nick looked around. "Where's Ruby?"

"She left when her phone rang, and she hasn't come back yet." Alexis stood on tiptoe, trying to see over the heads of the crowd. "If I feel bad about what we did, I can't imagine how she feels."

Nick rubbed the bruise on his temple where his head

had smacked into the man's nose. "I guess the whimpering I heard must have come from his dogs."

A man with a bristly crew cut lowered his binoculars and put his finger to his lips. Nick ground his teeth together and resisted the urge to punch him.

"I'm going to go find Ruby," he told Alexis. Part of him wanted to punch Ruby, too. It had been her crazy idea that the runner had been the killer. Her crazy idea that there was just one killer, a killer who was collecting homeless girls the way other people collected stamps.

Nick started pushing through the crowd, with Alexis following. He didn't care if he stepped on toes. He didn't care anymore about the black cloud of birds wheeling overhead. He didn't care about anything. He hadn't saved that tattooed girl from certain death. He hadn't saved her from anything except being kept home from partying. He wasn't a hero, the way he had always dreamed of being. He was just some stupid kid who had attacked an innocent man for no reason. It didn't matter that breaking that guy's nose had really been an accident. He had been happy enough to claim it when everyone had thought he had done it on purpose.

Now what would his dad think of him? Not much, he guessed.

They had reached the fringes of the crowd, but Nick still hadn't spotted Ruby. He wondered how she felt. She was the one who had been convinced she had come up with the solution, had put all the pieces together. What was she thinking now that she knew how wrong she had been?

When he reached the corner, Nick stopped, and

Alexis did, too. Where was Ruby? He looked up and down the shadowed streets. Finally, he spotted a flash of copper-colored hair. There. Two blocks away, going up the steep hill that led to Forest Park. Was it Ruby? He squinted. He was pretty sure it was. But who was that guy with her?

And then he caught a glimpse of a white beard and thick white hair and realized it was Becker. The bird-watcher. Only why did he have his arm under Ruby's elbow?

Alexis turned to him. "Is that Ruby? Where's she going? Why is she leaving with that man?"

Nick's thoughts were running through his brain like water, too fast for him to grab on to any single one. Ruby had said she and Alexis had talked to Becker in Forest Park the day Miranda was killed. Then he and Ruby had seen Becker there again on Sunday. And tonight he was here at Chapman school. Why did Becker keep turning up? And why was Ruby walking off with him now, when she was supposed to be with them? When she was supposed to be giving him and Alexis a ride to the sheriff's office soon?

He gave voice to his thoughts. "If the runner isn't the killer, then someone else who was in the park that day has to be. And I'm not talking about the homeless guy."

When he turned to Alexis, she was staring at him. Her mouth fell open. Then she grabbed his arm. "Oh no. It must be the birder. And he has Ruby." She shook his arm. "Nick, he has Ruby!"

The smartest thing was to stay put. To let the professionals handle it. Nick would call 9-1-1, and in five minutes, the police would be here.

But if Becker was planning on doing something bad, did Ruby even have five minutes? Nick thought of his dad. Outnumbered, outgunned, he had gone down fighting.

But his dad had had nothing to lose, a little voice said. It was one thing if you were going to die, no matter whether you fought back or not. Then why not go down swinging? Why not be a hero?

But if you had a choice, the way Nick did? Then the smart thing was to look after yourself first. To keep yourself safe. Not to do anything reckless.

Because if Becker was the killer, and Nick confronted him, if he tried to save Ruby, it was quite possible they would both end up dead at Becker's hands. There was no point in putting himself in danger.

In that split second, Nick made up his mind. And then he did the only thing he could do.

CHAPTER 43

WEDNESDAY

SEE FOR YOURSELF

THERE WAS NO SPOTTED OWL, OF COURSE. There never had been. But in a few minutes, he would point excitedly up into the trees and tell Ruby he had caught a glimpse of it. Right there!

Then he would offer the binoculars, inviting her to see for herself. As he had with the first girl, the one who had dropped his binoculars and nearly broken them. His anger had burst out, and when it subsided, everything had changed.

He would loop the strap over her neck before he handed them to her. And when Ruby tilted her head back, exposing the long white column of her throat, he would grab the strap in his fists and pull up and back. Pull so hard he would lift her from the ground. Her feet dancing in midair. Her weight against him as she struggled. And then ceased to struggle.

Just as he had done with the other girls.

Ruby would see, all right.

THE FLESH AGAINST HER BONES

A S SHE STARED AT THE FOOTPRINT, RUBY'S whole body went cold. For a moment, her thoughts straightened themselves into something like coherence. Had Becker seen her notice the pattern of chevrons and diamonds? Did he know she had seen that footprint before, next to a dead girl's body?

She had to get away from him.

"You know what?" It was an effort to enunciate, to put her tongue in the right places within the vast cave of her mouth. "I need to go back to the school. Alexis and Nick will be wondering where I am." Despite her concentration, her words still sounded smeared.

Before Ruby could turn back, Becker's hand was wrapped around her wrist, his grip so tight that even through her jacket, she could feel his fingers squeeze the flesh against her bones. He made a sound that was something like a laugh.

"Oh, it's fine, Ruby. We'll be back soon. And you don't want to miss your chance to see a real spotted owl.

It's been years since one's been seen here. We just need to go a little farther in."

He started moving forward, but she dug in her toes. "I changed my mind. I'll look at the owl some other time."

Becker stopped and turned back to face her. He had not released her wrist. Even though he was standing still, his face seemed to be moving toward her and then away. Ruby blinked and tried to focus. His eyes looked like chips of sea ice, and his face was set and stern.

"Come on, Ruby, we've come this far. It's just a little bit farther. You'll see. It's truly magnificent. The sighting of a lifetime."

"No. I don't think so." Ruby worked to make her words come out in the right order. "I really don't want to go with you. I want to go back to my friends now."

The muscles on either side of Becker's jaw bunched themselves. His lips pulled back from his gums, exposing long teeth. All pretense fell away. With his free hand, he pulled something black from the pocket of his pants. Ruby was still figuring out what it was when he thumbed it open, revealing it to be a folding knife. It was like watching a magic trick in a nightmare.

"I said you're coming with me." His voice was no louder than it had been, but now it held an edge as sharp as the knife's.

All Ruby could focus on was the blade as long as his hand, shining silver in the moonlight. She imagined the knife slipping over her throat, leaving behind a wet red smile. Or plunging into her gut and ripping up to her heart.

Becker was braced, waiting for her to pull away from him. Instead she stepped toward him, throwing him off balance. She kept his bulk between her and the point of the knife. At the same time, she twisted her wrist so that it pushed against the weakest part of his grip, his thumb.

With a curse, he was forced to let go of her arm. But Ruby's muddled brain hadn't made any further plans. What should she do now? Becker was standing between her and the way back out of the park. And if she ran farther down the trail, he would easily follow her.

So Ruby chose the third way.

HE'S GOING
TO KILL HER

"WAIT!" NICK HEARD ALEXIS CALLING OUT behind him. "Nick, wait up!" He ignored her. Even though he had never imagined ignoring Alexis, there was no time to wait. He had also never imagined seeing a man pull a knife on his friend.

Nick had a combat knife at home, bought off eBay. Sometimes he practiced with it in his room, grunting and thrusting it into the air, but he could not imagine ever using it on a person. Let alone a slight red-haired girl.

As he galloped up the hill, Nick held his phone up in front of him. It was hard to find the right button to push, not in the low light of the setting sun, not when he was running full tilt. He finally found the icon for the phone—almost tripping over a curb in the process—but when he pressed it, he didn't get the keypad on the next screen, just some words in a box. He squinted. They read RETURN CALL.

He pressed it, then held the phone to his ear, trying to quiet his breathing enough so he could hear.

The phone rang just once. Then the detective grunted, "Harriman."

"He's after Ruby," Nick gasped. "He's chasing her. I think he's going to kill her." He spoke in bursts, sucking air in between. He was still running flat out.

"I do not have the patience for this. Who is this? Who's after Ruby? Do you mean Ruby McClure?"

"It's Nick Walker. That birder guy, Becker"—Nick felt a fleeting sense of triumph at remembering the man's name—"Becker's chasing her. Into Forest Park. And he's got a knife."

INTO THE SHADOWS

WITH HER HANDS OUTSTRETCHED, RUBY ran into the shadowy darkness under the trees. It was impossible to be completely quiet, so she concentrated on putting as much distance as she could between herself and Becker. Night was falling, and she hoped that her dark clothes would provide some camouflage. As she lurched between trees, branches slapped her cheeks, tore at her hair, and plucked at the sleeves of her coat. She stumbled over the ground ridged with roots.

Ruby's thoughts should have been urgent, but they felt as soft and worn as old corduroy. She was thinking too slowly. Moving too slowly. Her legs didn't want to obey her. What had Becker put in that cocoa?

In a mostly futile effort to avoid getting scratched, she held her hands in front of her face. Gritting her teeth, she forced herself to keep hurtling forward, to ignore the little voice that told her to stop, to lie down, to give up.

She had to keep moving. She didn't have any choice. If she stopped, Becker would find her. He would find her and kill her. Just like he had killed those other girls.

But why her? She certainly wasn't Hispanic. Then a memory swam to the front of her mind. The clump of blond hair Nick had found on their evidence search. Now she realized that that hair had been cut, not pulled from Miranda Wyatt's head. So Becker had killed a girl with black kinky hair, a blond girl, and a girl with straight black hair.

And tonight he planned to add red hair to his collection. Her hair.

But not if she could help it. Ruby just hoped she was managing to hold on to some sense of direction. That she was running parallel to the border of the park, not deeper and deeper into its heart.

She didn't know how long she had been running. Ten minutes? Twenty? It was getting harder to churn forward. Wet ferns washed her pants. Her legs felt numb. Ruby caught her toe on a rock and fell headlong. She landed so hard that it forced the air from her lungs. For a long moment she lay stunned, until finally something loosened and she was able to suck in some air. It hurt nearly as much going in as it had going out, but the next breath came easier.

She was mentally yelling at herself to get to her feet when she realized she could hear—nothing. Nothing but the sounds of a nearby stream and faraway traffic. She held her breath. Still nothing.

Had she lost him, then? Or—and the idea sparked a distant fear in her—maybe he was only a few paces away, regarding her? Deciding the best place to slip in the knife?

Moving as quietly as possible, Ruby pushed herself up to her hands and knees. She turned her head from side to side, ignoring how everything seemed to ripple and shift. She was alone. She took a breath that sounded more like a sob.

Now what? Ruby decided to count to a hundred before she got to her feet. *One jelly bean, two jelly bean, three jelly bean.* Every fresh bruise ached, every scratch stung.

When she reached twenty-three jelly bean, a sound cut through the stillness. To her left, someone was crashing through the underbrush, but it sounded at least a block away.

Ruby had done it! She had lost Becker. She got to her feet and started to move as quietly as she could in the opposite direction. The sounds also seemed to be moving farther away.

Her heart lightening, Ruby rounded a big fir tree.

And realized how wrong she had been.

ALIVE TO HIS FINGERTIPS

WHEN RUBY HAD FIRST DARTED OFF, rabbited into the woods, a red rage had filled Becker. How dare she defy him? How dare she run off?

The other girls hadn't caused him any trouble. They had been unsuspecting. The first death had surprised even him.

So he had cursed when he had been forced to chase after Ruby. But as Becker pushed his way through brambles and bushes, he became aware of how strongly his heart was beating in his chest. Then he paused to listen for Ruby, to look for signs of her passing. As he sucked in a breath of sweet air, he realized he was alive to his fingertips. All his senses were working together to track her down.

This was, he realized, even better than those other times. What kind of challenge had they offered, really?

He wasn't the type of man who would buy a trip to one of those game farms where you shot unsuspecting exotic animals from twenty feet away as they placidly grazed. No. Man was meant to be a hunter. To match wits with his prey. The surrender was then all the more satisfying for the struggle.

He made himself move deliberately, rationally. Ruby was younger and fitter, but the GHB had leveled the playing field by affecting her thinking and coordination. And, of course, she still had the tracker on her. He took out his phone and found Ruby's tiny moving dot. And then he cut around and got in front of her.

Ah, and here she came now. Blundering right toward him. He flipped the knife closed and slipped it into his pocket. He would use it later.

But not just yet.

CHAPTER 48

WEDNESDAY

ONLY GOT WORSE

LEGS CHURNING, ALEXIS WAS DESPERATELY trying to keep up with Nick, but she kept falling farther behind. He was already way ahead. His legs were a blur, and he seemed undaunted by the steepness of the hill. Alexis felt like she was dying. Her knees hurt, her thighs burned, and there was a stabbing pain in her side that only got worse with each rasping breath.

And what was going to happen when they caught up to Becker and Ruby? How exactly were they supposed to save her, let alone protect themselves? Neither she nor Nick had anything resembling a weapon. Her Leatherman multipurpose tool was in her SAR backpack on her bedroom floor. Even if she'd had it, its tiny knife would have been dwarfed by Becker's, which had glinted in the light of the rising moon.

Becker's knife was scary enough. What if he had a gun?

What they needed, Alexis thought, was something they could use to hold him at bay. To hurt him, if need be. As she hurried up the hill—it was no longer quite a run; Alexis simply couldn't manage more than a sort of lurching trot—she scanned the yards she was passing, looking for something useful she could grab. Her frantic gaze found a ceramic pig on a porch, a loose brick on the sidewalk, a yellow recycling bin in a driveway, a hose coiled on a lawn, and a rose-covered wooden trellis against a house. She tried to imagine converting each into something she could use to hurt or even kill Becker. Tried—and failed.

Nick must have been thinking the same thing, because ahead of her he suddenly veered to the left and grabbed a rock as big as a cantaloupe from a garden. Clutching the rock to his chest, he disappeared into Forest Park.

CHAPTER 49

WEDNESDAY

TIME TO LET GO

RUBY ROUNDED A FIR TREE, PUSHED HER way through a blackberry bush, and entered a small clearing—where she came face-to-face with Becker.

He was holding his binoculars clasped to his chest. This did not seem terribly ominous.

Until he lunged forward and looped the strap around the back of her neck, jerking her forward.

His hands were fisted around the cord, which let the loose binoculars thump painfully against her ribs. The strap sawed into the back of her neck. Becker's face was only a few inches from hers. His breath was sour and rotten. He was close enough that she could knee him. But before Ruby could even complete the thought, he stepped behind her, the strap sliding sideways around her neck. Then he pulled it even tighter.

As the cord slipped around her neck, Ruby raised her left hand. She managed to hook two fingers between it and her neck just before it tightened across the front of her throat. The cord dug into her skin, pressing against her windpipe, squeezing her arteries and veins. Far from helping, her own knuckles were being forced against her throat, only increasing the pressure. She was making sounds she had never heard anyone make before, barking coughs and desperate gurgles. The sounds scared her as much as anything. They sounded like they were coming from someone who was dying.

With her free hand, Ruby frantically groped over her right shoulder, trying to find Becker's face. If only she could pull his hair, yank his nose, gouge his eyes! Anything so that she could take a breath. Take a breath and stop making those awful sounds.

Her scrabbling hand found nothing. In an effort to gain an inch or two, she arched her back and went up on her toes. Her lungs screamed silently for air as the cord sawed deeper into her neck.

Then Ruby's fingertips skimmed the skin of his cheek, brushed the edge of his shoulder. He grunted in surprise.

Yes! If she could just make him loosen his grip. She had to breathe. Her lungs were hollow with need.

But with one of his heavy hiking boots, Becker viciously kicked her calves. Pain shot from her Achilles tendons to the base of her spine. He kicked again. Ruby's cry of agony was stillborn, choked off along with her air.

He was, she realized, trying to knock her off her feet. If he succeeded, she would add her own weight to his. *Dead weight*, Ruby thought, as the strap sliced into her fingers, into her throat. She would be dead weight.

Her vision spun like water swirling down a drain.

"That's it," Becker murmured into Ruby's ear as her struggle began to slow. "That's it, Ruby. Let go."

She stopped fighting. Stopped trying to breathe.

"It's time to let go now," he whispered. So gently. He kissed her temple.

Her vision tilted. The moon spun in the sky. The world darkened, then dwindled to nothing.

Ruby's knees sagged. Everything went black.

CRY OUT IN HORROR

NICK SPRINTED UP THE TRAIL, RUNNING AS fast as he ever had in his life. At what he thought was the same spot where he had seen Ruby and Becker disappear, he plunged into the woods. He ran flat out for a few minutes, branches slashing at him, then stopped to listen, trying to hold his breath. There. A noise. To his left.

He darted forward, but when he stopped again a minute later, he heard nothing. Nothing. His heart was a bird trapped in the cage of his ribs. Where was Ruby? Was he too late? Had Becker already found her? Found her and killed her?

There—did Nick hear noises to his right? He started running again, somehow managing to keep to his feet even when he tripped over a root. And then he heard it. Someone was choking and coughing. The sound let him know both that Ruby was alive and that she wouldn't be for long.

He found them in a little clearing. But Ruby was on the ground. On the ground and unmoving, her face slack.

Holding the knife, Becker was leaning over her body. Nick cried out in horror.

The older man spun around. In his hand, the wicked-looking knife glinted silver. When he saw Nick, the corners of his mouth lifted, but it wasn't a smile. It was a thing he did with his mouth.

With a banshee yell, Nick threw the heavy rock right at Becker's head.

And watched the other man duck. The rock sailed over his shoulder and thudded harmlessly on the ground.

Leaving Nick with nothing but empty hands.

He closed them into fists and leapt forward, swinging wildly at Becker, trying to drive him away from Ruby.

Becker pulled his right fist over his head and then hammered down, punching Nick in the shoulder.

At least it felt like a punch. But why was the knife no longer silver when Becker pulled back his hand? And why did Nick's chest and belly suddenly feel hot and wet? Then he looked down and saw the blood. So much blood. In the fading light, it looked almost black.

Nick dropped to his knees. He just needed a minute to figure things out.

While he was trying to make sense of it all, the ground suddenly rushed up to meet him.

THREE BODIES

AT THE EDGE OF THE CLEARING, ALEXIS stopped short. What she saw turned her bones to water.

Her two friends were sprawled on the forest floor. Ruby's fingers were curled against her throat, and Nick was covered with blood. Neither one was moving.

Becker was standing over them, his face a twisted mask of fury. He hadn't yet seen Alexis. He was concentrating on kicking Nick's head with one of his hiking boots.

He was pulling his leg back to do it again when Alexis darted up behind him and swung the heavy wooden handle of the rake she had snatched from a lawn. It hit Becker's head with a hollow, sickening crunch, making a sound like a melon falling off a kitchen table.

And that was how the police found Alexis Frost. Holding a rake like a baseball bat, with three bodies around her, blood spattered over the leaves, and tears running down her face.

LIKE BIRDS

"YOU SURE YOU'RE UP FOR SAR TONIGHT?"
Alexis asked Nick as the three of them waited for
Detective Harriman. It was the same interview room
where she had picked out the photo of Jay Adams less
than two weeks ago. As soon as investigators got a look
inside Caleb Becker's house, Adams had been released.
"Jon said it was okay if we missed class again."

All three of them had missed last week's class, of
course. About the time it began, Alexis was being interviewed by the police, and both Nick and Ruby were being
rushed to the hospital. For that matter, so was Caleb
Becker, although it was a different one and he had a
police officer stationed outside his door.

Now Nick nodded. "I don't want to miss two weeks
in a row. Besides, I'm doing good." Then he winced and
put his hand to his shoulder. He wore a button-down
flannel shirt with the top three buttons undone to reveal
layers and layers of gauze.

Was Alexis a terrible person for wondering if the
wince and the bandages were a touch exaggerated? She

probably was, given that just a week ago she had been convinced that Nick was dead.

Instead, after Becker had stabbed him, Nick had fainted. That part got left out of his version of events, and who was Alexis to contradict him? He had still rushed a serial killer empty-handed. He had still needed twenty-six stitches.

And Ruby? She claimed she had been playing dead to fool Becker. To Alexis's eyes, she had actually been pretty darn dead, or close to it. A week later, Ruby's voice was still hoarse from her bruised larynx. The red mark on her throat where the strap of the binoculars had dug into her was slowly fading.

"I still wish you had hit Becker's head hard enough to kill him," Nick said now.

"I don't." Alexis shivered. "I'd have to live with that forever." If she had nightmares now, what would they be like if they featured a real-life dead man?

"In the army, they'd call that a righteous kill."

"I don't care what anyone would call it. It would still be killing someone. I just wanted to knock him out, and that's what I did." Although really Alexis hadn't been thinking about either knocking out Becker or killing him. She had just wanted everything to stop. To finally stop.

Alexis, Nick, and Ruby had spent the last few days talking to cops, being interviewed by Detective Harriman, and being alternately lectured and hugged by their parents. Alexis's mom cut out stories about them from the *Oregonian* and *USA Today* and pasted them into her scrapbooks. A few days later, Alexis, Nick, and Ruby had even been featured in *People* magazine. Each article was garbled in different ways. Even Alexis wasn't exactly sure what the truth was. She had a feeling it would take months to untangle. And maybe it would never be straightened out. Who could understand a man who had collected girls like birds?

In the past week, a few threads had been teased out.

Caleb Becker was a software engineer who didn't have any close friends. Just acquaintances who were also birders. A year earlier, he had volunteered with a wildlife biologist who was trapping birds and fitting them with tracking devices. The biologist had told Detective Harriman that Becker even wrote a computer program to better follow the birds' movements. Later, he had used a version of the same program to track homeless girls.

No one was exactly sure when or why he had moved on from birds to girls, but his church had provided volunteers for a soup kitchen once a month, and other volunteers remembered his curiosity about the homeless people they served.

The door to the interview room opened, and Detective Harriman walked in. If anything, he looked even more wrinkled and tired than usual. He was lugging a cardboard banker's box, which he plopped with a sigh in the middle of the table. Then he took a seat.

His face reddened as he looked at them each in turn. "I have to apologize to you guys. You were right about it not being Jay Adams. I should have listened to you."

While Alexis murmured acceptance and Nick nodded, Ruby said bluntly, "You've been doing your job for a long time. Maybe you've gotten stuck in a rut."

Alexis pressed her lips together so she wouldn't burst out laughing.

The muscles in Harriman's jaw flexed as if he was biting his tongue. Hard. He took a deep breath and then said, "Becker still isn't talking to us. We're hoping you three can help fill in some of the blanks."

They all nodded.

"We do know some things, and we're guessing on some others. Like we believe the three girls who have been found are the only ones he killed."

"How do you know that?" Ruby demanded.

"Because in his house we found three clippings of hair tied with ribbon. And they match the known victims."

"That must have been what Nick found at the evidence search," Ruby said. "Some of the hair he clipped off Miranda's head."

"That's right."

Alexis exhaled in relief. With luck, that meant there weren't any more bodies lying under trees in secluded green spaces. Waiting for SAR to gather up their bones. She had been so worried about Raina, but Alexis had finally learned that she had returned to her family.

"Another reason we believe there were only three victims is that we found photos of the three girls—taken after they were dead—in Caleb Becker's den." Across from Alexis, Nick made a face. "We also found numerous photos of birds and framed displays of feathers."

"Those are illegal," Ruby said.

"I'm sure after killing three people, Becker was really worried about the Migrant Bird Act," Nick said.

"Migratory," Ruby corrected, and for once Alexis found herself smiling instead of gritting her teeth. Ruby might be weird, but she was their kind of weird.

Harriman took the lid off the box, then reached in and brought out a small blue notebook. It had been slipped into a plastic bag, opened to a page in the middle so that you could see both sides. He pushed it toward them. They all leaned forward. At the top was printed *A Birding Journal*. The handwriting was small and crabbed, but Alexis persevered until it became clear.

SPECIES NAME
Homeless, also known as street people, hobos, bums, drifters.

INDIVIDUAL SPECIMEN
Tiffany Yee, aged 17.

Alexis could read only a few lines before her gorge rose. She put her hand over mouth and closed her eyes. In her mind, though, she could still see the sketch on the opposite page. It was nearly unrecognizable, not much more than a stick figure. But still, it was clearly not a bird.

"Alexis found that notebook on the day we found the body," Ruby said. "And then Becker came up and asked for it back."

"You told me it was a birding notebook," Alexis said from behind the shelter of her hand. "I even saw a drawing like that, but I just remember thinking he was a really bad artist." She hadn't even disagreed with Ruby. If she had, then maybe Tiffany Yee would still be alive. "We just found it and gave it back to him."

"We believe the notebook fell out of his pocket when he killed Miranda Wyatt," Harriman said. "We think he gave her GHB in alcohol, just as he gave it to Ruby in cocoa, and then walked with her into the park."

"I smelled it!" Ruby exclaimed. "When I leaned over her, she kind of smelled like my dad does when he has a drink after dinner."

Harriman nodded. "GHB makes people compliant. Maybe he pulled the same trick on Miranda that he did on you, Ruby, and told her they were going to see a spotted owl. Whatever ruse he used, we recovered DNA from Becker as well as four individuals on the strap of his binoculars: Ruby's, Miranda's, Tiffany's, and the girl who was found in Washington Park. And we now know that girl's name. It's DeShaundra Young. She was a runaway from San Diego. We think she's the first one he killed."

"So she was a girl," Ruby said. "Not a woman?"

Harriman's face reddened. "She was eighteen. But she'd already had her wisdom teeth out."

"But why did he kill her? DeShaundra?" Nick asked. "Why did he kill any of them?"

"It's possible the first death was an accident," Harriman said. "Maybe he was trying to get her to look at a bird through the binoculars and she resisted or argued or wasn't sufficiently impressed. For some people, killing causes an incredible high. And after that, the only way to get that high is to do it again."

Alexis felt sick. When she had believed Becker was

dead, all she had felt was horror at what she had done. She couldn't imagine looking forward to doing it again.

"He also had dozens of loose photos of girls," Harriman added. "Live girls, not dead ones. All of them with different colors and types of hair. Because of that and the clippings, we believe it was hair color he used to pick his victims, not skin color. So you got it right, Ruby. Mostly."

"But not right enough," Ruby said. "He told me that in humans, females had the most interesting plumage. I should have figured it out then."

Alexis realized she wasn't the only one feeling guilty.

Harriman reached into the box again. "So, Ruby, these are the photos we have of you. Do you know when they were taken?" Harriman slid them over, each in a plastic sleeve. Alexis didn't recognize the pictures as coming from any specific event, but Ruby and Nick did.

"It's from the day we met him in Forest Park," Ruby said. "He must have taken some photos of us before we saw him."

"He's the one who told us about the swifts," Nick added.

"He also seems to have put some kind of tracker on other girls and on you, Ruby." Harriman said. "We found printouts showing your location at various times. They started on Sunday."

"That explains how he found me in Forest Park," Ruby said. "Nick and I talked to him on Sunday, but I don't—" She turned to Nick. "Wait, do you remember how he lost his balance and had to grab on to me for support?" She dumped the contents of her coat pockets onto the table— car keys and more gum wrappers than Alexis had ever seen in one place. Harriman was telling her to wait, but before he had finished speaking, she was pulling something from a small compartment in her backpack.

"What's this?" Ruby said. "It's not mine."

"Put it down!" Harriman ordered, and Ruby let it fall onto the table. "We might still be able to get prints." Using the edge of a file folder, he scooted it away from her.

"Do you really need to worry about that?" Alexis asked. "After all, you found this guy with Nick's blood on his knife and his binoculars still wrapped around Ruby's neck. And both of them can testify as to what he did to them."

"You ever heard that expression: put another nail in the coffin?" Detective Harriman smiled grimly. "I want as many nails as possible."

SYMMETRICAL

B Y THE TIME RUBY AND THE OTHERS WERE
done talking to Detective Harriman, there wasn't
enough time to go home before they were due at the
sheriff's office for class. After pooling their money—well,
it was mostly Ruby's money, but she didn't mind—they
bought dinner at a nearby McDonald's.

Ruby ordered what she always did at McDonald's: a
Filet-O-Fish, an empty cup for water, and a large order of
fries. Now she was methodically eating her fries, con-
suming each one in three bites, no more and no less, dip-
ping them into ketchup before each bite.

"You're like a machine," Nick observed.

Distracted by the sight of her own reflection in the
window behind him, Ruby didn't answer. She always
wondered how she looked to others. Red hair, pale skin,
big blue eyes. Was she pretty? About all she could tell was
that she was symmetrical.

"She's just being logical," Alexis said. "Right, Ruby?"

"I like patterns," Ruby said.

"If it weren't for your patterns"—Alexis raised her

paper cup like she was toasting Ruby—"the cops would never have caught Becker."

"That only happened because you guys believed me." Ruby next said what she normally only thought. "Most people just think I'm weird."

"Well, you are," Nick said. "But so are me and Alexis. And who said being weird is a bad thing?" Putting his hand to his mouth, he only half smothered a burp. "The three of us are like what you said. About what Becker wanted."

Alexis's features bunched up. "What are you talking about, Nick?"

But Ruby knew. "He was collecting the set."

Nick pointed a fry at her. "Exactly. That's like us. We're different, but we fit together."

"So we're each, like, a type?" Alexis asked. "I assume you're talking about more than our hair."

"We've got the smart girl"—Nick pointed at Ruby— "the pretty girl"—his finger moved on to Alexis—"and the"—he pointed to himself and hesitated—"the brave guy."

Alexis jabbed her own finger at him. "Hey, I'm a lot more than just the pretty girl."

"If it weren't for Alexis, both of us would be dead," Ruby said.

As it was, the doctors had insisted on keeping Ruby in the hospital overnight, which had freaked her out nearly as badly as her confrontation with Becker. She figured the sickest people within a hundred miles were right there in the same building, breathing the same air and generally spreading their germs. She had eventually talked one of the nurses into bringing her a roll of tape, and she had spent a half hour taping Kleenexes over anything she might have to touch, including light switches, door handles, and the flushing mechanism for the toilet.

"But I was sure it was the homeless guy," Alexis said. "And it turned out that he had nothing to do with it. Just some creepy guy who liked to hit on women."

"Speaking of homeless, did your parents get mad that you spent the night in a homeless shelter?" Nick asked.

"It's just my mom." Alexis looked down and pressed her lips together. "And no, she didn't."

Ruby thought she looked sad. She wanted to console her friend but had no idea how to. How could she make Alexis feel better? How could she show she cared? She didn't want to play Supportive Best Friend; she wanted to be it. But how? Ruby's shoulders got tight as her confusion grew. She forced herself to take a deep breath, to suspend analysis and critical thinking. No matter what Nick said, sometimes people didn't really want logic.

Instead Ruby pushed over her red and yellow box. "Want the rest of my fries?

And was rewarded with Alexis's smile.

FOAM HEART

FROM UNDER HER EYELASHES, ALEXIS watched Bran as he waited at Perk Up's counter for Mara to finish making their coffees. She didn't know what it meant that he had wanted to get together again, or if it meant anything at all. He had texted and called several times to see how she was doing.

Probably his interest was professional. Poor Alexis, he must be thinking, what with having a bipolar mom, finding a dead body, and nearly killing a killer. He must think she needed a lot of trauma intervention.

The strange thing was that, although she had done her best to kill Becker, Alexis didn't hate him. Maybe she even had some twisted sympathy for him after living with her mom and her mom's mental illness all these years.

Now Bran came back to their table carrying two lattes. After looking from one glass to the other, he slid one over to her. "It's my lucky day. The latte art is doing my speaking for me."

His had a leaf. But hers was decorated with a white foam heart.

A flush climbed her cheeks. He *must* like her. She tried to think of a reply but couldn't.

"After all, you're a hero," Bran said. "And everyone loves a hero."

Suddenly Alexis was very glad she hadn't thought of anything the slightest bit romantic to say. "I didn't feel like a hero," she said honestly. "I was just scared. The worst thing was that I thought it was all over. That Ruby and Nick were already dead, so it didn't matter. None of it mattered."

"So you three must be pretty good friends? I didn't pick that up that first night."

Friends? But Alexis realized it was true. "We've been through a lot together since then. To be honest, I've never had that many friends. We've always moved around a lot. And I didn't want people to know about my mom." She took a long sip, then set down her glass.

Bran did the same, leaving behind a faint mustache of foam. Then he reached across the table and took her hand. "I hope you have room for one more."

Alexis was still cautious. "You mean friend?"

His face turned red. "And more. But only if you want."

For an answer, Alexis leaned forward. And in front of Mara and a dozen other patrons, she kissed the foam right off Bran's lips.

ACKNOWLEDGMENTS

About two years ago, some friends told me that their daughter volunteered for Multnomah County Sheriff's Office Search and Rescue (MCSO SAR). Not only did she help find people lost in the woods, but she also searched for crime scene evidence and recovered scattered remains. As they spoke, I knew immediately this was the idea I had long sought: the basis for a realistic mystery series. In this book, I have called my group Portland County Sheriff's Office Search and Rescue, but it was inspired by MCSO SAR.

In MCSO SAR, teens aren't just observers. In fact, all the leadership positions are held by teens. While adult members are allowed, they aren't on a separate team. Youth are the team leaders on real searches, and they do not require adult oversight. The other thing that makes MCSO SAR unusual is that about one-third of the time they are called out to assist law enforcement by searching for crime scene evidence.

So thanks go to Sarah Roberts for volunteering with MCSO SAR and for her parents, Nancy and Brock Roberts, for telling me about it. Sarah in turn introduced me to Jake Keller, the group's training adviser, who has patiently answered dozens of questions, from the type of knife a character might carry to what he or she would say over the radio. Isabel LaCourse, another member since her teens, also graciously answered my queries.

For research that doesn't involve SAR, Lee Lofland, who runs the one and only Writers Police Academy, has been a font of wisdom. The Crime Scene Writers Group on Yahoo also offers a great place to gather accurate information. And Joe Liebezeit, Avian Conservation Program manager for the Audubon Society, helped me put the right birds in Forest Park.

Thanks to my editor, Christy Ottaviano, for immediately seeing the potential in Alexis, Nick, and Ruby. Other wonderful folks at Henry Holt include Amy Allen, April Ward, Holly Hunnicutt, Allison Verost, Molly Brouillette, Ksenia Winnicki, Marianne Cohen, Lucy Del Priore, and Emily Waters. And this is the seventeenth book that my amazing agent, Wendy Schmalz, and I have done together.